HOW
WE
GOT
INSIPID

HOW

WE

GOT

INSIPID

Jonathan Lethem

Subterranean Press • 2006

First Edition

ISBN
1-59606-054-9

Subterranean Press
PO Box 190106
Burton, MI 48519

www.subterraneanpress.com

HOW WE GOT
IN TOWN
AND OUT AGAIN

When we first saw somebody near the mall Gloria and I looked around for sticks. We were going to rob them if they were few enough. The mall was about five miles out of the town we were headed for, so nobody would know. But when we got closer Gloria saw their vans and said they were scapers. I didn't know what that was, but she told me.

It was summer. Two days before this Gloria and I had broken out of a pack of people that had food but we couldn't stand their religious chanting anymore. We hadn't eaten since then.

"So what do we do?" I said.

"You let me talk," said Gloria.

"You think we could get into town with them?"

"Better than that," she said. "Just keep quiet."

I dropped the piece of pipe I'd found and we walked in across the parking lot. This mall was long past being good for finding food anymore but the scapers were taking out folding chairs from a store and strapping them on top of their vans. There were four men and one woman.

"Hey," said Gloria.

Two guys were just lugs and they ignored us and kept lugging. The woman was sitting in the front of the van. She was smoking a cigarette.

The other two guys turned. This was Kromer and Fearing, but I didn't know their names yet.

"Beat it," said Kromer. He was a tall squinty guy with a gold tooth. He was kind of worn but the tooth said he'd never lost a fight or slept in a flop. "We're busy," he said.

He was being reasonable. If you weren't in a town you were nowhere. Why talk to someone you met nowhere?

But the other guy smiled at Gloria. He had a thin face and a little mustache. "Who are you?" he said. He didn't look at me.

"I know what you guys do," Gloria said. "I was in one before."

"Oh?" said the guy, still smiling.

"You're going to need contestants," she said.

"She's a fast one," this guy said to the other guy. I'm Fearing," he said to Gloria.

"Fearing what?" said Gloria.

"Just Fearing."

"Well, I'm just Gloria."

"That's fine," said Fearing. "This is Tommy Kromer. We run this thing. What's your little friend's name?"

"I can say my own name," I said. "I'm Lewis."

"Are you from the lovely town up ahead?"

"Nope," said Gloria. "We're headed there."

"Getting in exactly how?" said Fearing.

"Anyhow," said Gloria, like it was an answer. "With you, now."

"That's assuming something pretty quick."

"Or we could go and say how you ripped off the last town and they sent us to warn about you," said Gloria.

"Fast," said Fearing again, grinning, and Kromer shook his head. They didn't look too worried.

"You ought to want me along," said Gloria. "I'm an attraction."

"Can't hurt," said Fearing.

Kromer shrugged, and said, "Skinny, for an attraction."

"Sure, I'm skinny," she said. "That's why me and Lewis ought to get something to eat."

Fearing stared at her. Kromer was back to the van with the other guys.

"Or if you can't feed us—" started Gloria.

"Hold it, sweetheart. No more threats."

"We need a meal."

"We'll eat something when we get in." Fearing said. "You and Lewis can get a meal if you're both planning to enter."

"Sure," she said. "We're gonna enter—right Lewis?"

I knew to say right.

———— ▪■●■▪ ————

The town militia came out to meet the vans, of course. But they seemed to know the scapers were coming, and after Fearing talked to them for a couple of minutes they opened up the doors and had a quick look then waved us through. Gloria and I were in the back of a van with a bunch of equipment and one of the lugs, named Ed. Kromer drove. Fearing drove the van with the woman in it. The other lug drove the last one alone.

I'd never gotten into a town in a van before, but I'd only gotten in two times before this anyway. The first time by myself, just by creeping in, the second because Gloria went with a militia guy.

Towns weren't so great anyway. Maybe this would be different.

We drove a few blocks and a guy flagged Fearing down. He came up to the window of the van and they talked, then went back to his car, waving at Kromer on his way. Then we followed him.

"What's that about?" said Gloria.

"Gilmartin's the advance man." said Kromer. "I thought you knew everything,"

Gloria didn't talk. I said, "What's an advance man?"

"Gets us a place, and the juice we need," said Kromer. "Softens the town up. Gets people excited."

It was getting dark. I was pretty hungry, but I didn't say anything. Gilmartin's car led us to this big building shaped like a boathouse only it wasn't near any water. Kromer said it used to be a bowling alley.

The lugs started moving stuff and Kromer made me help. The building was dusty and empty inside, and some of the lights didn't work. Kromer said just to get things inside for now. He drove away one of the vans and came back and we unloaded a bunch of little cots that Gilmartin the advance man had rented, so I had an idea where I was going to be sleeping. Apart from that it was stuff for the contest. Computer cables and plastic spacesuits, and loads of televisions.

Fearing took Gloria and they came back with food, fried chicken and potato salad, and we all ate. I couldn't stop going back for more but nobody said anything. Then I went to sleep on a cot. No one was talking to me. Gloria wasn't sleeping on a cot. I think she was with Fearing.

———— ▪●▪ ————

Gilmartin the advance man had really done his work. The town was sniffing around first thing in the morning. Fearing was out talking to them when I woke up. "Registration begins at noon, not a minute sooner," he was saying. "Beat the lines and stick around. Well be serving coffee. Be warned, only the fit need apply—our doctor will be examining you, and he's never been fooled once. It's Darwinian logic, people. The future is for the strong. The meek will have to inherit the here and now."

Inside, Ed and the other guy were setting up the gear. They had about thirty of those wired-up plastic suits stretched out in the middle of the place, and so tangled up with cable and little wires that they were like husks of fly bodies in a spiderweb.

Under each of the suits was a light metal frame, sort of like a bicycle with a seat but no wheels, but with a headrest too. Around the web they were setting up the televisions in an arc facing the seats. The suits each had a number on the back, and the televisions had numbers on top that matched.

When Gloria turned up she didn't say anything to me but she handed me some donuts and coffee.

"This is just the start," she said, when she saw my eyes get big. "We're in for three squares a day as long as this thing lasts. As long as we last, anyway."

We sat and ate outside where we could listen to Fearing. He went on and on. Some people were lined up like he said. I didn't blame them since Fearing was such a talker. Others listened and just got nervous or excited and went away, but I could tell they were coming back later, at least to watch. When we finished the donuts Fearing came over and told us to get on line too.

"We don't have to," said Gloria.

"Yes, you do," said Fearing.

On line we met Lane. She said she was twenty like Gloria but she looked younger. She could have been sixteen, like me.

"You ever do this before?" asked Gloria.

Lane shook her head. "You?"

"Sure," said Gloria. "You ever been out of this town?"

"A couple of times," said Lane. "When I was a kid. I'd like to now."

"Why?"

"I broke up with my boyfriend."

Gloria stuck out her lip, and said, "But you're scared to leave town, so you're doing this instead."

Lane shrugged.

I liked her, but Gloria didn't.

The doctor turned out to be Gilmartin the advance man. I don't think he was a real doctor, but he listened to my heart. Nobody ever did that before, and it gave me a good feeling.

Registration was a joke, though. It was for show. They asked a lot of questions but they only sent a couple of women and one guy away, Gloria said for being too old. Everyone else was okay, despite how some of them looked pretty hungry, just like me and Gloria. This was a hungry town. Later I figured out that's part of why Fearing and Kromer picked it. You'd think they'd want to go where the money was, but you'd be wrong.

After registration they told us to get lost for the afternoon. Everything started at eight o'clock.

———·—·•—·—·———

We walked around downtown but almost all the shops were closed. All the good stuff was in the shopping center and you had to show a town ID card to get in and me and Gloria didn't have those.

So, like Gloria always says, we killed time since time was what we had.

———— ▪■●■▪ ————

The place looked different. They had spotlights pointed from on top of the vans and Fearing was talking through a microphone. There was a banner up over the doors. I asked Gloria and she said "Scape-Athon." Ed was selling beer out of a cooler and some people were buying, even though he must have just bought it right there in town for half the price he was selling at. It was a hot night. They were selling tickets but they weren't letting anybody in yet. Fearing told us to get inside.

Most of the contestants were there already. Anne, the woman from the van, was there, acting like any other contestant. Lane was there too and we waved at each other. Gilmartin was helping everybody put on the suits. You had to get naked but nobody seemed to mind. Just being contestants made it all right, like we were invisible to each other.

"Can we be next to each other?" I said to Gloria.

"Sure, except it doesn't matter," she said. "We won't be able to see each other inside."

"Inside where?" I said.

"The scapes," she said. "You'll see."

Gloria got me into my suit. It was plastic with wiring everywhere and padding at my knees and wrists and elbows and under my arms and in my crotch. I tried on the mask but it was heavy and I saw nobody else was wearing theirs so I kept it off until I had to. Then Gilmartin tried to help Gloria but she said she could do it herself.

So there we were, standing around half naked and dripping with cable in the big empty lit-up bowling alley, and then suddenly Fearing and his big voice came inside and they let the people in and the lights went down and it all started.

"Thirty-two young souls ready to swim out of this world, into the bright shiny future," went Fearing. "The question is, how far into that future will their bodies take them? New worlds are theirs for the taking—a cornucopia of scapes to boggle and amaze and gratify the senses. These lucky kids will be immersed in an ocean of data overwhelming to their undernourished sensibilities—we've assembled a really brilliant collection of environments for them to explore—and you'll be able to see everything they see, on the monitors in front of you. But can they make it in the fast lane? How long can they ride the wave? Which of them will prove able to outlast the others, and take home the big prize—one thousand dollars? That's what we're here to find out."

Gilmartin and Ed were snapping everybody into their masks and turning all the switches to wire us up and getting us to lie down on the frames. It was comfortable on the bicycle seat with your head on the headrest and a belt around your waist. You could move your arms and legs like you were swimming, the way Fearing said. I didn't mind putting on the mask now because the audience was making me nervous. A lot of them I couldn't see because of the lights, but I could tell they were there, watching.

The mask covered my ears and eyes. Around my chin there was a strip of wire and tape. Inside it was dark and quiet at first except Fearing's voice was still coming into the earphones.

"The rules are simple. Our contestants get a thirty minute rest period every three hours. These kids'll be well fed, don't worry about that. Our doctor will monitor their health. You've heard the horror stories, but we're a class outfit: you'll see no horrors here. The kids earn the quality care we provide one way: continuous, waking engagement with the data stream. We're firm on that. To sleep is to die—you can sleep on your own time, but not ours. One lapse, and you're out of the game—them's the rules."

The earphones started to hum. I wished I could reach out and hold Gloria's hand, but she was too far away.

"They'll have no help from the floor judges, or one another, in locating the perceptual riches of cyberspace. Some will discover the keys that open the doors to a thousand worlds, others will bog down in the antechamber to the future. Anyone caught coaching during rest periods will be disqualified—no warnings, no second chances."

Then Fearing's voice dropped out, and the scapes started.

———— ▪▫●▫▪ ————

I was in a hallway. The walls were full of drawers, like a big cabinet that went on forever. The drawers had writing on them that I ignored. First I couldn't move except my head, then I figured out how to walk, and just did that for a while. But I never got anywhere. It felt like I was walking in a giant circle, up the wall, across the ceiling, and then back down the other wall.

So I pulled open a drawer. It only looked big enough to hold some pencils or whatever but when I pulled it opened like a door and I went through.

"Welcome to Intense Personals," said a voice. There were just some colors to look at. The door closed behind me. "You must be eighteen years of age or older to use this service. To avoid any charges, please exit now."

I didn't exit because I didn't know how. The space with colors was kind of small except it didn't have any edges. But it felt small.

"This is the main menu. Please reach out and make one of the following selections: women seeking men, men seeking women, women seeking women, men seeking men, or alternatives."

Each of them was a block of words in the air. I reached up and touched the first one.

"After each selection touch *one* to play the recording again, *two* to record a message for this person, or *three* to advance to the next selection. You may touch three at any time to advance to the next selection, or four to return to the main menu."

Then a woman came into the colored space with me. She was dressed up and wearing lipstick.

"Hi, my name is Kate," she said. She stared like she was looking through my head at something behind me and poked at her hair while she talked. "I live in San Francisco. I work in the financial district, as a personnel manager, but my real love is the arts, currently painting and writing—"

"How did you get into San Francisco?" I said.

"—just bought a new pair of hiking boots and I'm hoping to tackle Mount Tam this weekend," she said, ignoring me.

"I never met anyone from there," I said.

"—looking for a man who's not intimidated by intelligence," she went on. "It's important that you like what you do, like where you are. I also want someone who's confident enough that I can express my vulnerability. You should be a good listener—"

I touched three. I can read numbers.

Another woman came in, just like that. This one was as young as Gloria, but kind of soft-looking.

"I continue to ask myself why in the *heck* I'm doing this personals thing," she said, sighing. "But I know the reason—I want to date. I'm new to the San Francisco area. I like to go to the theater, but I'm really open-minded. I was born and raised in Chicago, so I think I'm a little more east coast than west. I'm fast-talking and cynical. I guess I'm getting a little cynical about these ads, the sky has yet to part, lightning has yet to strike—"

I got rid of her, now that I knew how.

"—I have my own garden and landscape business—"

"—someone who's fun, not nerdy—"

"—I'm tender, I'm sensuous—"

I started to wonder how long ago these women were from. I didn't like the way they were making me feel, sort of guilty and bullied at the same time. I didn't think I could make any of them happy the way they were hoping but I didn't think I was going to get a chance to try, anyway.

It took pretty long for me to get back out into the hallway. From then on I paid more attention to how I got into things.

The next drawer I got into was just about the opposite. All space and no people. I was driving an airplane over almost the whole world, as far as I could tell. There was a row of dials and switches under the windows but it didn't mean anything to me. First I was in the mountains and I crashed a lot, and that was dull because a voice would lecture me before I could start again, and I had to wait. But then I got to the desert and I kept it up without crashing much. I just learned to say "no" whenever the voice suggested something different like "engage target" or "evasive action." I wanted to fly awhile, that's all. The desert looked good from up there, even though I'd been walking around in deserts too often.

Except that I had to pee I could have done that forever. Fearing's voice broke in, though, and said it was time for the first rest period.

———— ▬ ● ▬ ————

"—still fresh and eager after their first plunge into the wonders of the future," Fearing was saying to the people in the seats. The place was only half full. "Already this world seems drab by comparison. Yet, consider the irony, that as their questing minds grow accustomed to these splendors, their bodies will begin to rebel—"

Gloria showed me how to unsnap the cables so I could walk out of the middle of all that stuff still wearing the suit, leaving the mask behind. Everybody lined up for the bathroom. Then we went to the big hall in the back where they had the cots, but nobody went to sleep or anything. I guessed we'd all want to next time, but right now I was too excited and so was everybody else. Fearing just kept talking like us taking a break was as much a part of the show as anything else.

"Splendors, hah," said Gloria. "Bunch of second-hand cyber junk."

"I was in a plane," I started.

"Shut up," said Gloria. "We're not supposed to talk about it. Only, if you find something you like, remember where it is."

I hadn't done that, but I wasn't worried.

"Drink some water," she said. "And get some food."

They were going around with sandwiches and I got a couple, one for Gloria. But she didn't seem to want to talk.

Gilmartin the fake doctor was making a big deal of going around checking everybody even though it was only the first break. I figured that the whole point of taking care of us so hard was to remind the people in the seats that they might see somebody get hurt.

Ed was giving out apples from a bag. I took one and went over and sat on Lane's cot. She looked nice in her suit.

"My boyfriend's here," she said.

"You're back together?"

"I mean ex-. I'm pretending I didn't see him."

"Where?"

"He's sitting right in front of my monitor." She tipped her head to point.

I didn't say anything but I wished I had somebody watching me from the audience.

———— ▪▬●▬▪ ————

When I went back the first thing I got into was a library of books. Every one you took off the shelf turned into a show, with charts and pictures, but when I figured out that it was all business stuff about how to manage your money, I got bored.

Then I went into a dungeon. It started with a wizard growing me up from a bug. We were in his workshop, which was all full of jars and cobwebs. He had a face like a melted candle and he talked as much as Fearing. There were bats flying around.

"You must resume the quest of Kroyd," he said to me and started touching me with his stick. I could see my arms and legs, but they weren't wearing the scaper suit. They were covered with muscles. When the wizard touched me I got a sword and a shield. "These are your companions, Rip and Batter," said the wizard. "They will obey you and protect you. You must never betray them for any other. That was Kroyd's mistake."

"Okay," I said.

The wizard sent me into the dungeon and Rip and Batter talked to me. They told me what to do. They sounded a lot like the wizard.

We met a Wormlion. That's what Rip and Batter called it. It had a head full of worms with little faces and Rip and Batter said to kill it, which wasn't hard. The head exploded and all the worms started running away into the stones of the floor like water.

Then we met a woman in sexy clothes who was holding a sword and shield too. Hers were loaded with jewels and looked a lot nicer than Rip and Batter. This was Kroyd's mistake, anyone could see that. Only I figured Kroyd wasn't here and I was, and so maybe his mistake was one I wanted to make too.

Rip and Batter started screaming when I traded with the woman, and then she put them on and we fought. When she killed me I was back in the doorway to the Wizard's room, where I first ran in, bug-sized. This time I went the other way, back to the drawers.

Which is when I met the snowman.

I was looking around in a drawer that didn't seem to have anything in it. Everything was just black. Then I saw a little blinking list of numbers in the corner. I touched the numbers. None of them did anything except one.

It was still black but there were five pictures of a snowman. He was three balls of white, more like plastic than snow. His eyes were just o's and his mouth didn't move right when he talked. His arms were sticks but they bent like rubber. There were two pictures of him small and far away, one from underneath like he was on a hill and one that showed the top of his head, like he was in a hole. Then there was a big one of just his head, and a big one of his whole body. The last one was of him looking in through a window, only you couldn't see the window, just the way it cut off part of the snowman.

"What's your name?" he said.

"Lewis."

"I'm Mr. Sneeze." His head and arms moved in all five pictures when he talked. His eyes got big and small.

"What's this place you're in?"

"It's no place," said Mr. Sneeze. "Just a garbage file."

"Why do you live in a garbage file?"

"Copyright lawyers," said Mr. Sneeze. "I made them nervous." He sounded happy no matter what he was saying.

"Nervous about what?"

"I was in a Christmas special for interactive television. But at the last minute somebody from the legal department thought I looked too much like a snowman on a video game called *Mud Flinger.* It was too late to redesign me so they just cut me out and dumped me in this file."

"Can't you go somewhere else?"

"I don't have too much mobility." He jumped and twirled upside down and landed in the same place, five times at once. The one without a body spun too.

"Do you miss the show?"

"I just hope they're doing well. Everybody has been working so hard.

I didn't want to tell him it was probably a long time ago.

"What are you doing here, Lewis?" said Mr. Sneeze.

"I'm in a Scape-Athon."

"What's that?"

I told him about Gloria and Fearing and Kromer, and about the contest. I think he liked that he was on television again.

———— ▪■●■▪ ————

There weren't too many people left in the seats. Fearing was talking to them about what was going to happen tomorrow when they came back, Kromer and Ed got us all in the back. I looked over at Lane's cot. She was already asleep. Her boyfriend was gone from the chair out front.

I lay down on the cot beside Gloria. "I'm tired now," I said.

"So sleep a little," she said, and put her arm over me. But I could hear Fearing outside talking about a "Sexathon" and I asked Gloria what it was.

"That's tomorrow night," she said. "Don't worry

about it now." Gloria wasn't going to sleep, just looking around.

———— ▬■●■▬ ————

I found the SmartHouse Showroom. It was a house with a voice inside. At first I was looking around to see who the voice was but then I figured out it was the house.

"Answer the phone!" it said. The phone was ringing.

I picked up the phone, and the lights in the room changed to a desk light on the table with the phone. The music in the room turned off.

"How's that for responsiveness?"

"Fine," I said. I hung up the phone. There was a television in the room, and it turned on. It was a picture of food. "See that?"

"The food, you mean?" I said.

"That's the contents of your refrigerator!" it said. "The packages with the blue halo will go bad in the next twenty-four hours. The package with the black halo has already expired! Would you like me to dispose of it for you?"

"Sure."

"Now look out the windows!"

I looked. There were mountains outside.

"Imagine waking up in the Alps every morning!"

"I—"

"And when you're ready for work, your car is already warm in the garage!"

The windows switched from the mountains to a picture of a car in a garage.

"And your voicemail tells callers that you're not home when it senses the car is gone from the garage!"

I wondered if there was somewhere I could get if I went down to drive the car. But they were trying to sell me this house, so probably not.

"And the television notifies you when the book you're reading is available this week as a movie!"

The television switched to a movie, the window curtains closed, and the light by the phone went off.

"I can't read," I said.

"All the more important, then, isn't it?" said the house.

"What about the bedroom?" I said. I was thinking about sleep.

"Here you go!" A door opened and I went in. The bedroom had another television. But the bed wasn't right. It had a scribble of electronic stuff over it.

"What's wrong with the bed?"

"Somebody defaced it," said the house. "Pity."

I knew it must have been Fearing or Kromer who wrecked the bed because they didn't want anyone getting that comfortable and falling asleep and out of the contest. At least not yet.

"Sorry!" said the house. "Let me show you the work center!"

———— -■●■- ————

Next rest I got right into Gloria's cot and curled up and she curled around me. It was real early in the morning and nobody was watching the show now and Fearing wasn't talking. I think he was off taking a nap of his own.

Kromer woke us up. "He always have to sleep with you, like a baby?"

Gloria said, "Leave him alone. He can sleep where he wants."

"I can't figure," said Kromer. "Is he your boyfriend or your kid brother?"

"Neither," said Gloria. "What do you care?"

"Okay," said Kromer. "We've got a job for him to do tomorrow, though."

"What job?" said Gloria. They talked like I wasn't there.

"We need a hacker boy for a little sideshow we put on." said Kromer "He's it."

"He's never been in a scape before," said Gloria. "He's no hacker."

"He's the nearest we've got. We'll walk him through it."

"I'll do it," I said.

"Okay, but then leave him out of the Sexathon," said Gloria.

Kromer smiled. "You're protecting him? Sorry. Everybody plays in the Sexathon, sweetheart. That's bread and butter. The customers don't let us break the rules." He pointed out to the rigs. "You'd better get out there."

I knew Kromer thought I didn't know about Gloria and Fearing, or other things. I wanted to tell him I wasn't so innocent, but I didn't think Gloria would like it, so I kept quiet.

———— ▪■●■▪ ————

I went to talk to Mr. Sneeze. I remembered where he was from the first time.

"What's a Sexathon?" I said.

"I don't know, Lewis."

"I've never had sex," I said.

"Me neither," said Mr. Sneeze.

"Everybody always thinks I do with Gloria just because we go around together. But we're just friends."

"That's fine," said Mr. Sneeze. "It's okay to be friends."

"I'd like to be Lane's boyfriend," I said.

———— ▪■●■▪ ————

Next break Gloria slept while Gilmartin and Kromer told me about the act. A drawer would be marked for me to go into, and there would be a lot of numbers and letters but I just had to keep pressing "1-2-3" no matter what. It was supposed to be a security archive, they said. The people watching would think I was breaking codes but it was just for show. Then something else would happen but they wouldn't say what, just that I should keep quiet and let Fearing talk. So I knew they were going to put me out of my mask. I didn't know if I should tell Gloria.

Fearing was up again welcoming some people back in. I couldn't believe anybody wanted to start watching first thing in the morning but Fearing was saying "the gritty determination to survive that epitomizes the frontier spirit that once made a country called America great" and "young bodies writhing in agonized congress with the future" and that sounded like a lot of fun, I guess.

A woman from the town had quit already. Not Lane though.

———— ▄▄●▄▄ ————

A good quiet place to go was Mars. It was like the airplane, all space and no people, but better since there was no voice telling you to engage targets, and you never crashed.

———— ▄▄●▄▄ ————

I went to the drawer they told me about. Fearing's voice in my ear told me it was time. The place was a storeroom of information like the business library. No people, just files with a lot of blinking lights and complicated words. A voice kept asking me for "security clearance password" but there was always a place for me to touch "1-2-3" and I did. It was kind of a joke, like a wall made out of feathers that falls apart every time you touch it.

I found a bunch of papers with writing. Some of the words were blacked out and some were bright red and blinking. There was a siren sound. Then I felt hands pulling on me from outside and somebody took off my mask.

There were two guys pulling on me who I had never seen before, and Ed and Kromer were pulling on them. Everybody was screaming at each other but it was kind of fake, because nobody was pulling or yelling very hard. Fearing said "The feds, the feds!" A bunch of people were crowded around my television screen I guess looking at the papers I'd dug up, but now they were watching the action.

Fearing came over and pulled out a toy gun and so did Kromer, and they were backing the two men away from me. I'm sure the audience could tell it was fake. But they were pretty excited, maybe just from remembering when feds were real.

I got off my frame and looked around. I didn't know what they were going to do with me now that I was out but I didn't care. It was my first chance to see what it was like when the contestants were all in their suits and masks, swimming in the information. None of them knew what was happening, not even Gloria, who was right next to me the whole time. They just kept moving in the scapes. I looked at Lane. She looked good, like she was dancing.

Meanwhile Fearing and Kromer chased those guys out the back. People were craning around to see. Fearing came out and took his microphone and said. "It isn't his fault, folks. Just good hacker instincts for ferreting out corruption from encrypted data. The feds don't want us digging up their trail, but the kid couldn't help it."

Ed and Kromer started snapping me back into my suit. "We chased them off," Fearing said, patting his gun. "We do take care of our own. You can't tell who's going to come sniffing around, can you? For his protection and ours we're going to have to delete that file, but it goes to show, there's no limit to what a kid with a nose for data's going to root out of cyberspace. We can't throw him out of the contest for doing what comes natural. Give him a big hand, folks."

People clapped and a few threw coins. Ed picked the change up for me, then told me to put on my mask. Meanwhile Gloria and Lane and everybody else just went on through their scapes.

I began to see what Kromer and Fearing were selling. It wasn't any one thing. Some of it was fake and some was real, and some was a mix so you couldn't tell.

The people watching probably didn't know why they wanted to, except it made them forget their screwed-up lives for a while to watch the only suckers bigger than themselves—us.

"Meanwhile, the big show goes on," said Fearing. "How long will they last? Who will take the prize?"

———— ▪■●■▪ ————

I told Gloria about it at the break. She just shrugged and said to make sure I got my money from

Kromer. Fearing was talking to Anne the woman from the van and Gloria was staring at them like she wanted them dead.

A guy was lying in his cot talking to himself as if nobody could hear and Gilmartin and Kromer went over and told him he was kicked out. He didn't seem to care.

I went to see Lane but we didn't talk. We sat on her cot and held hands. I didn't know if it meant the same thing to her that it did to me but I liked it

After the break I went and talked to Mr. Sneeze. He told me the story of the show about Christmas. He said it wasn't about always getting gifts. Sometimes you had to give gifts too.

———— ▪■●■▪ ————

The Sexathon was late at night. They cleared the seats and everyone had to pay again to get back in, because it was a special event. Fearing had built it up all day, talking about how it was for adults only, it would separate the men from the boys, things like that. Also that people would get knocked out of the contest. So we were pretty nervous by the time he told us the rules.

"What would scapes be without virtual sex?" he said. "Our voyageurs must now prove themselves in the sensual realm—for the future consists of far more than cold, hard information. It's a place of desire and temptation, and, as always, survival belongs to the fittest. The soldiers will now be steered onto the sexual battlescape—the question is, will they meet with the Little Death, or the Big one?"

Gloria wouldn't explain. "Not real death," is all she said.

"The rules again are so simple a child could follow them. In the Sex-Scape environment our contestants will be free to pick from a variety of fantasy partners. We've packed this program with options, there's something for every taste, believe you me. We won't question their selections, but—here's the catch—we will chart the results. Their suits will tell us who does and doesn't attain sexual orgasm in the next session, and those who don't will be handed their walking papers. The suits don't lie. Find bliss or die, folks, find bliss or die."

"You get it now?" said Gloria to me.

"I guess," I said.

"As ever, audience members are cautioned never to interfere with the contestants during play. Follow their fantasies on the monitors, or watch their youthful bodies strain against exhaustion, seeking to bridge virtual lust and bona fide physical response. But no touchee."

Kromer was going around, checking the suits. "Who's gonna be in your fantasy, kid?" he said to me. "The snowman?"

I'd forgotten how they could watch me talk to Mr. Sneeze on my television. I turned red.

"Screw you, Kromer," said Gloria.

"Whoever you want, honey," he said, laughing.

Well I found my way around their Sex-Scape and I'm not too embarrassed to say I found a girl who reminded me of Lane, except for the way she was trying so hard to be sexy. But she looked like Lane. I didn't have to do much to get the subject around to sex. It was the only thing on her mind. She wanted me to tell her what I wanted to do to her and when I couldn't think of much she suggested things and I just agreed. And when I did that she would move around and sigh as if it were really exciting to talk about even though she was doing the talking. She wanted to touch me but she couldn't really so she took off her clothes and got close to me and touched herself. I touched her too but she didn't really feel like much and it was like my hands were made of wood, which couldn't have felt too nice for her though she acted like it was great.

I touched myself a little too. I tried not to think about the audience. I was a little confused about what was what in the suit and with her breathing in my ear so loud but I got the desired result. That wasn't hard for me.

Then I could go back to the drawers but Kromer had made me embarrassed about visiting Mr. Sneeze so I went to Mars even though I would have liked to talk to him.

———— ▪▪●▪▪ ————

The audience was all stirred up at the next break. They were sure getting their money's worth now. I got into Gloria's cot. I asked her if she did it with her own hands too. "You didn't have to do that," she said.

"How else?"

"I just pretended. I don't think they can tell. They just want to see you wiggle around."

Well some of the women from the town hadn't wiggled around enough I guess because Kromer and Ed were taking them out of the contest. A couple of them were crying.

"I wish I hadn't," I said.

"It's the same either way," said Gloria. "Don't feel bad. Probably some other people did it too."

They didn't kick Lane out but I saw she was crying anyway.

Kromer brought a man into the back and said to me, "Get into your own cot, little snowman."

"Let him stay," said Gloria. She wasn't looking at Kromer.

"I've got someone here who wants to meet you," said Kromer to Gloria "Mr. Warren, this is Gloria."

Mr. Warren shook her hand. He was pretty old. "I've been admiring you," he said. "You're very good."

"Mr. Warren is wondering if you'd let him buy you a drink," said Kromer.

"Thanks, but I need some sleep," said Gloria.

"Perhaps later," said Mr. Warren.

After he left Kromer came back and said, "You shouldn't pass up easy money."

"I don't need it," said Gloria. "I'm going to win your contest, you goddamn pimp."

"Now, Gloria," said Kromer. "You don't want to give the wrong impression."

"Leave me alone."

I noticed now that Anne wasn't around in the rest area and I got the idea that the kind of easy money Gloria didn't want Anne did. I'm not so dumb.

———— ▬▬●▬▬ ————

Worrying about the Sexathon had stopped me from feeling how tired I was. Right after that I started nodding off in the scapes. I had to keep moving around. After I'd been to a few new things I went to see the snowman again. It was early in the morning and I figured Kromer was probably asleep and there was barely any audience to see what I was doing on my television. So Mr. Sneeze and I talked and that helped me stay awake.

I wasn't the only one who was tired after that night. On the next break I saw that a bunch of people had dropped out or been kicked out for sleeping. There were only seventeen left. I couldn't stay awake myself. But I woke up when I heard some yelling over where Lane was.

It was her parents. I guess they heard about the Sexathon, maybe from her boyfriend, who was there too. Lane was sitting crying behind Fearing who was telling her parents to get out of there, and her father just kept saying "I'm her father! I'm her father!" Her mother was pulling at Fearing but Ed came over and pulled on her.

I started to get up but Gloria grabbed my arm and said, "Stay out of this."

"Lane doesn't want to see that guy," I said.

"Let the townies take care of themselves, Lewis. Let Lane's daddy take her home if he can. Worse could happen to her."

"You just want her out of the contest," I said.

Gloria laughed. "I'm not worried about your girl-friend outlasting me," she said. "She's about to break no matter what."

So I just watched. Kromer and Ed got Lane's parents and boyfriend pushed out of the rest area, back toward the seats. Fearing was yelling at them, making a scene for the audience. It was all part of the show as far as he was concerned.

Anne from the van was over talking to Lane, who was still crying, but quiet now.

"Do you really think you can win?" I said to Gloria.

"Sure, why not?" she said. "I can last."

"I'm pretty tired." In fact my eyeballs felt like they were full of sand.

"Well if you fall out stick around. You can proba-bly get food out of Kromer for cleaning up or some-thing. I'm going to take these bastards."

"You don't like Fearing anymore," I said.

"I never did," said Gloria.

———— ▪■●■▪ ————

That afternoon three more people dropped out. Fearing was going on about endurance and I got think-ing about how much harder it was to live the way me and Gloria did than it was to be in town and so maybe we had an advantage. Maybe that was why Gloria thought she could win now. But I sure didn't feel it myself. I was so messed up that I couldn't always sleep at the rest periods, just lie there and listen to Fearing or eat their sandwiches until I wanted to vomit.

Kromer and Gilmartin were planning some sideshow but it didn't involve me and I didn't care. I didn't want coins thrown at me. I just wanted to get through.

———— ▬■●■▬ ————

If I built the cities near the water the plague always killed all the people and if I built the cities near the mountains the volcanoes always killed all the people and if I built the cities on the plain the other tribe always came over and killed all the people and I got sick of the whole damn thing.

"When Gloria wins we could live in town for a while," I said. "We could even get jobs if there are any. Then if Lane doesn't want to go back to her parents she could stay with us."

"You could win the contest," said Mr. Sneeze.

"I don't think so," I said. "But Gloria could."

———— ▬■●■▬ ————

Why did Lewis cross Mars? To get to the other side. Ha ha.

———— ▪■●■▪ ————

I came out for the rest period and Gloria was already yelling and I unhooked my suit and rushed over to see what was the matter. It was so late it was getting light outside and almost nobody was in the place. "She's cheating!" Gloria screamed. She was pounding on Kromer and he was backing up because she was a handful mad. "That bitch is cheating! You let her sleep!" Gloria pointed at Anne from the van. "She's lying there asleep, you're running tapes in her monitor you goddamn cheater!"

Anne sat up in her frame and didn't say anything. She looked confused. "You're a bunch of cheaters!" Gloria kept saying. Kromer got her by the wrists and said "Take it easy, take it easy. You're going scape-crazy, girl."

"Don't tell me I'm crazy!" said Gloria. She twisted away from Kromer and ran to the seats. Mr. Warren was there, watching her with his hat in his hands. I ran after Gloria and said her name but she said "Leave me alone!" and went over to Mr. Warren. "You saw it, didn't you?" she said.

"I'm sorry?" said Mr. Warren.

"You must have seen it, the way she wasn't moving at all," said Gloria. "Come on, tell these cheaters you saw it. I'll go on that date with you if you tell them."

"I'm sorry, darling. I was looking at you."

Kromer knocked me out of the way and grabbed Gloria from behind. "Listen to me, girl. You're hallucinating.

You're scape-happy. We see it all the time." He was talking quiet but hard. "Any more of this and you're out of the show, you understand? Get in the back and lie down now and get some sleep. You need it."

"You bastard," said Gloria.

"Sure, I'm a bastard, but you're seeing things." He held Gloria's wrist and she sagged.

Mr. Warren got up and put his hat on. I'll see you tomorrow, darling. Don't worry. I'm rooting for you." He went out.

Gloria didn't look at him.

Kromer took Gloria back to the rest area but suddenly I wasn't paying much attention myself. I had been thinking Fearing wasn't taking advantage of the free action by talking about it because there wasn't anyone much in the place to impress at this hour. Then I looked around and I realized there were two people missing and that was Fearing and Lane.

I found Ed and I asked him if Lane had dropped out of the contest and he said no.

———— ▬▬●▬▬ ————

"Maybe there's a way you could find out if Anne is really scaping or if she's a cheat," I said to Mr. Sneeze.

"I don't see how I could," he said. "I can't visit her, she has to visit me. And nobody visits me except you." He hopped and jiggled in his five places. "I'd like it if I could meet Gloria and Lane."

"Let's not talk about Lane," I said.

———— ▪■●■▪ ————

When I saw Fearing again I couldn't look at him. He was out talking to the people who came by in the morning, not in the microphone but one at a time, shaking hands and taking compliments like it was him doing the scaping.

There were only eight people left in the contest. Lane was still in it but I didn't care.

I knew if I tried to sleep I would just lie there thinking. So I went to rinse out under my suit, which was getting pretty rank. I hadn't been out of that suit since the contest started. In the bathroom I looked out the little window at the daylight and I thought about how I hadn't been out of that building for five days either, no matter how much I'd gone to Mars and elsewhere.

I went back in and saw Gloria asleep and I thought all of a sudden that I should try to win.

But maybe that was just the idea coming over me that Gloria wasn't going to.

———— ▪■●■▪ ————

I didn't notice it right away because I went to other places first. Mr. Sneeze had made me promise I'd always have something new to tell him about so I always opened a few drawers. I went to a tank game but it was boring. Then I found a place called the American History Blood And Wax Museum and I stopped President Lincoln from getting murdered a couple of times. I tried to stop President Kennedy from getting murdered but if I stopped it one way it always happened a different way. I don't know why.

So then I was going to tell Mr. Sneeze about it and that's when I found out. I went into his drawer and touched the right numbers but what I got wasn't the usual five pictures of the snowman. It was pieces of him but chopped up and stretched into thin white strips, around the edge of the black space, like a band of white light.

I said, "Mr. Sneeze?"

There wasn't any voice.

I went out and came back in but it was the same. He couldn't talk. The band of white strips got narrower and wider, like it was trying to move or talk. It looked a bit like a hand waving open and shut. But if he was still there he couldn't talk.

I would have taken my mask off then anyway, but the heat of my face and my tears forced me to.

I saw Fearing up front talking and I started for him without even getting my suit unclipped, so I tore up a few of my wires. I didn't care. I knew I was out now. I went right out and tackled Fearing from behind. He wasn't so big, anyway. Only his voice was big. I got him down on the floor.

"You killed him," I said, and I punched him as hard as I could, but you know Kromer and Gilmartin were there holding my arms before I could hit him more than once. I just screamed at Fearing, "You killed him, you killed him."

Fearing was smiling at me and wiping his mouth. "Your snowman malfunctioned, kid."

"That's a lie!"

"You were boring us to death with that snowman, you little punk. Give it a rest, for chrissake."

I kept kicking out even though they had me pulled away from him. "I'll kill you!" I said.

"Right," said Fearing. "Throw him out of here."

He never stopped smiling. Everything suited his plans, that was what I hated.

Kromer the big ape and Gilmartin pulled me outside into the sunlight and it was like a knife in my eyes. I couldn't believe how bright it was. They tossed me down in the street and when I got up Kromer punched me, hard.

Then Gloria came outside. I don't know how she found out, if she heard me screaming or if Ed woke her. Anyway she gave Kromer a pretty good punch in the side and said "Leave him alone!"

Kromer was surprised and he moaned and I got away from him. Gloria punched him again. Then she turned around and gave Gilmartin a kick in the nuts and he went down. I'll always remember in spite of what happened next that she gave those guys a couple they'd be feeling for a day or two.

———— ▪■●■▪ ————

The gang who beat the crap out of us were a mix of the militia and some other guys from the town, including Lane's boyfriend. Pretty funny that he'd take out his frustration on us, but that just shows you how good Fearing had that whole town wrapped around his finger.

Outside of town we found an old house that we could hide in and get some sleep. I slept longer than Gloria. When I woke up she was on the front steps rubbing a spoon back and forth on the pavement to make a sharp point, even though I could see it hurt her arm to do it.

"Well, we did get fed for a couple of days," I said.

Gloria didn't say anything.

"Let's go up to San Francisco," I said. "There's a lot of lonely women there."

I was making a joke of course.

Gloria looked at me. "What's that supposed to mean?"

"Just that maybe I can get us in for once."

Gloria didn't laugh, but I knew she would later.

THE INSIPID PROFESSION OF JONATHAN HORNEBOM

(HOMMAGE HEINLEIN)

1.

It was nearly dark. Jonathan Hornebom rushed along the sidewalk of Fourth Street, toward Barrow, terrified. He had to get home and see if the awful thing had recurred. He jostled a pair of tie-loosened businessmen as they strolled away from the subway, and nearly knocked into a teenager who was attempting to climb the curb with a skateboard. "Watch it, dude—"

"Sorry," muttered Hornebom as the teenager clacked away.

At Barrow Street he fumbled open his ironwork gate and went into the entrance under the stoop, to his studio. He pushed past the old canvases, those that had already received the damaging marks and those that had escaped, to the easel on the back wall, where his newest work sat covered. He pulled the sheet aside and then recoiled in horror.

The child in the foreground was just as he'd painted it. Eyes wide and shimmering, brimming with tears. The background, a field of flowers, was intact. But the sky—across his soft blue and white sky was another of the horrendous shapes, a terrifying black cyclone of bones and tendons. A bird-beast, with shining black eyes that mocked those of the child.

The shapes were, as always, painted into his work flawlessly, as if by his own hand. Indeed, he had to suspect his own hand, for want of other suspects.

But the additions were unimaginably gruesome, visions he could barely stomach, let alone originate.

The changes in the paintings forced him to confront the gaps in memory that made a patchwork of his days. He'd tried to ignore the inconsistencies. What was the importance of a lost hour, now and again? Amnesia he could live with. But if he was capable of committing these unspeakable desecrations of his work, what else might he be doing during the missing hours?

Or could there actually be a hidden tormentor, some mastermind capable of timing his attacks on the paintings to coincide with Hornebom's blackouts?

Enough! He had to know.

2.

Harriet was about to close up the office and go upstairs to her apartment when the phone rang. She thought about letting the machine pick it up anyway, and then she thought about her bank balance and reached for the receiver.

"I—is this Harriet M. Welch, the investigator?" The voice had a slight German accent.

"Right," she said.

"My name is Jonathan Hornebom. I'd like to talk to you, if I could."

"Talk."

"I—I'd rather—"

"You mean in person."

"Could I? Your office address is quite near."

"I'll be here for another half an hour," she said, putting her feet back up on the desk. She opened her drawer and took out the catalog that had come that day from Wily E.'s Surveillance Supplies and a half tomato sandwich left over from her lunch.

When Hornebom pressed the doorbell she buzzed him in without looking up, but when he entered the room she pushed the catalog into the trash basket along with the sandwich wrapping. The products were crap. She smiled up at Hornebom and said: "Mind if I smoke?"

"No, no," he said, and shook his head.

She lit a cigarette. "Sit down." She watched him put himself in the seat across her desk. He was younger than she'd guessed, but seeing his primness and reserve she understood her mistake. He was dressed like a character actor, in a gray suit, cravat, white gloves and a bowler. His hair was white but it still covered his head, and his pinched, severe features were overwhelmed by his eyes. They were deep-set, ringed, and huge. An eagle's eyes, if he'd met her gaze. Instead they darted away.

"What can I do for you, Mr. Hornebom?"

"I—I can't explain. I'm afraid it may be the stupidest thing you've ever heard—"

"That's a contest you can't hope to win. What's the problem? A woman? A business arrangement that's soured?"

"I have blackouts," Hornebom managed.

Harriet frowned. "You drink?"

"Never."

"I'm not a doctor."

"I'm not looking for one, not yet at least. I need to know what goes on during my—missing time. Because something's happened to my work."

"Your work?"

"I'm a painter. And someone, or something, is changing my work while I'm...out."

"Changing how?" Harriet stubbed out her cigarette, not sure whether she was intrigued or annoyed.

"Adding to my paintings—terrible things."

"Okay, wait a minute. You make a living from painting?" Her skepticism showed in her voice. He didn't look the type.

"Well, yes."

"So you're good. Or famous, anyway. Because you have to be, to make a living from art, right?"

"I...have a reputation."

She worked the story out of him. He lived alone, in his own brownstone, his studio in the basement apartment. (She upped her fee mentally.) The gaps in his memory were not in themselves disruptive. He'd find himself in the park, or in front of his television, or seated in a restaurant, with no memory of how he'd gotten there. But never anywhere unexpected, or unlikely.

Then, two weeks ago, he'd returned to his studio to find the first of the alterations. Nightmarish beaked and taloned things looming in his skies. Defacements, but expert ones. Either some ingenious tormentor with more knowledge of Hornebom's comings and goings than he himself possessed was destroying his work or, more horrifying to contemplate, he was destroying it himself.

"I want to be followed," Hornebom concluded. "I want you to track me like a suspect in a crime. Find out what I do, where I go. I'll pay for a full report. And if it's not me committing the artistic atrocities—"

"Would you want them arrested?"

He shuddered. "Report to me first, please. Let me decide."

"Does anyone else have a key to the studio?"

Hornebom shook his head. "My housekeeper has the upstairs key. But there's no interior stair. It was designed as a separate apartment. I have the only key."

"I'll need a copy," Harriet said. She was captivated now by the problem, the logistics. The possibility that Hornebom was merely insane she shunted to a rear part of her brain; she wanted a puzzle to solve, a locked-room mystery, and she wanted more of the checks that Hornebom now wrote out so readily with his trembling, gloved hands, one for her first day of work, and one as a standing retainer. She wanted a series of them, to pad the lining of her hemorrhaging bank account.

Assuming the first one didn't bounce, that was. He was as seedy as he was dandified, and from what Harriet had seen of the young, MTV-fresh SoHo art scene, Hornebom couldn't cut it in that crowd.

He agreed to bring her a copy of the key in the morning, and to slide it under her door if she was not in. What she didn't say was that she meant to be on his tail by then. The guy was nervous enough as it was.

3.

He started with coffee and pastry at an Italian bakery on Sixth Avenue, then walked uptown until he found a locksmith's. She followed him back to her office, where he rang, waited, and finally slipped the copied key under her door.

Then back to Barrow Street. He went downstairs, into the studio, and she set up with a newspaper on a stoop across the street. It was a nice enough day to be paid to kill time on the prettiest street in Manhattan.

When he emerged again, an hour later, she ducked down behind her paper. He swiveled on his heel and strode up the street, at twice his previous speed. She gave him half a block and started after, quelling a pang of curiosity about the studio itself. She still didn't have a key in hand, and anyway, he looked like a man on a mission.

Her heart was pounding. The old game, still magic. Just give me someone to follow, she thought, and I'm a kid again.

On Seventh he hailed a cab. She jumped into the street and grabbed the next one, commanding the driver to follow. He raised his eyebrows but didn't say anything. Hornebom's cab shot uptown, jerking through traffic, catching stretches of timed lights, then squeaking to a stop every block for six or seven red lights in a row, and Harriet's followed. Several times they swam together in block-long seas of identical yellow cabs, and Harriet had to help the driver stick to Hornebom's. They crossed town at Fifty-third Street and finally pulled to the curb in front of the Museum of Modern Art. Hornebom paid his driver and sped into the lobby of the building, and Harriet had to surrender a twenty in her haste to follow. Six-dollar tip, but she'd charge it all to Hornebom.

She pushed through the crowds milling in the outer lobby just in time to catch sight of him paying for his ticket and passing on into the museum. Fair enough; painter wants to look at paintings. Was he in his blackout phase? She couldn't know. She got in line for a ticket and watched him heading up a packed escalator.

She handed over her ticket and hurried through the turnstile, but the escalator was too crowded for her to do anything but stand still and wait her turn, and when she got to the top he was nowhere to be seen. She ducked into the permanent collection, a labyrinth of gigantic paintings that seemed to Harriet mostly flat fields of bright color, and scouted the rooms, searching for a glimpse of his white hair. He was not there.

She took the escalator up another floor. The exhibition was labeled "Anxious Furniture: Surrealist and Dada Objects and Sculpture 1916-1948," and it seemed to be what had drawn the crowds. Perhaps it had drawn Hornebom. She jostled her way into the first of the rooms. The admirers of the vast paintings downstairs had had to stand in the middle of the rooms to take in their full scope, but the displays here were in glass cases and were mostly quite small, so the crowds bunched tight around them. Harriet found it completely annoying. She wanted to poke the groups apart to see if Hornebom was hiding in among them. Instead she bumped her way around from behind, trying to ignore the inanely reverent comments. She didn't know anything about anxious furniture, but she had the distinct feeling she was in a room full of jokes being taken seriously.

She was ready to declare him lost and go back to explore his studio when suddenly there he was, standing still in a stream of moving bodies, in front of one of the glass cases. She let a few people pass and then found a place in the group around him, a few heads back. Standing up on her toes, she looked over his shoulder.

There were three objects in the case. On the left a teacup, saucer and spoon, all normally proportioned, but covered completely in fur. On the right a metronome topped with an eye, or a photograph of an eye, and otherwise unaltered. In the middle was an object that seemed a combination printing press and toy cannon: two-foot-high wheels with a complex assembly of rollers and handles suspended between them, and a gun barrel pointing out at the viewer.

Hornebom stood alone, seemingly frozen there, while groups filled in around him, and trickled away to be replaced again, and again. Harriet began to think he was in blackout mode now, whether or not he had been on his way up here. But no, Harriet suddenly noticed, Hornebom *wasn't* alone. Another man stood as an island in the stream of oglers. He was young, a few years younger than Harriet, with a little beard that did more to reveal his age than to hide it. He had set up a little to one side of the case, and was staring intently at the exhibit.

Harriet watched as the younger man became aware of Hornebom, who was planted so conspicuously in front of the case. She melted back farther into the crowd, to watch without the risk of being noticed herself. The younger man squinted at Hornebom as though recognizing him, then, looking back at the case, took out a small spiral-bound notebook and began jotting notes with a pencil.

Harriet reflexively patted at the notebook she kept in the kangaroo pocket of her sweatshirt.

The younger man went on writing, staring at the objects in the case, and occasionally glancing up at Hornebom. Hornebom remained seemingly oblivious, his gaze fixed on the middle object in the case.

Suddenly self-conscious of her participation in their odd threesome, she shuffled along to the next case, and followed the flow around the adjacent room, glancing back every few minutes to confirm Hornebom's presence. Finally she allowed herself to risk losing him, and finished the loop of the exhibition, which deposited her back at the entrance.

She peered in: they were both still there. She started in again, and nonchalantly scooted up behind the young man with the beard. In his notebook was a sketch of the cannon/printing press. He looked up suddenly, and around; she turned her head the other way and walked quickly off.

As for Hornebom, an hour had passed since she'd followed him into the museum, and still he stood entranced.

She went downstairs and, keeping her eye on the flow through the exit gates, leafed through the exhibition catalog on the gift counter. She found photographs of all three of the objects in the case. The teacup was labeled "Breakfast in Fur," by Meret Oppenheim. The metronome was "Object of Destruction," by Man Ray. And the device in the middle—the one the man with the beard had been sketching—was "Bird Camera," by Max Ernst.

Harriet was hungry, and tired of the museum. She went and found the sandwich counter in the courtyard, turning her back, for the moment, on the exit. If Hornebom escaped she'd go back downtown and check his house, and if he wasn't home she could inspect the studio. A good plan: she treated herself to roast beef and a large Coke, on the client.

By the time she was done the crowd had thinned. She went upstairs. At first she thought they were both gone, then she spotted the bearded man, sitting on a bench across the room from the glass case.

He looked up, and for the second time she had to turn quickly to keep from meeting his eyes. Sloppy, she chided herself. She scooted into the next room, then turned and looked back. He was gone from the bench. Well, never mind. It was Hornebom she should be troubling with. Where was he?

"Hello."

She turned around to find the young man with the beard standing before her, smiling.

"Hello," she said.

"Are you with the security staff?" he asked, still smiling pleasantly.

"What?"

"Here at the museum."

"No, no. Excuse me." She craned her neck around, worrying that Hornebom was in the room.

"Because you seem to be watching me or following me or something."

"Not you. Forget it."

"The old guy, then. The one staring at the Ernst thing."

"Quiet," she commanded. They were attracting attention.

"He left, if that's what you're worried about. So, if you weren't following me, would you have coffee with me?"

"Shhh. I—I just had a Coke. Where did he go? No, don't talk. Let's go downstairs."

They made their way to the garden. Harriet led him to a table in the farthest corner, and sat so that she commanded a view of the entire yard behind him.

"You don't work for the museum either," she suggested.

"Nope. I'm Rich, uh, Richard DeBronk. I'm a student. A graduate student, I mean. At Hunter."

Professional loafer, Harriet supplied to herself. It fit his bumbling manner, and her suspicions of him eased. "Well, I'm Harriet Welch," she said. "What do you know about the man you saw today, Mr. DeBronk?"

"What do I know about—Well, what do *you* know, I mean, why should I tell you? If you're not working for the museum, what are you doing asking me questions?"

"You asked me out, Richard. This is a *date.* This is my feeble conversational tack. Have you ever seen that man before?"

DeBronk assumed a thoughtful pose. "I don't think so." He squinted at Harriet. "But he did look kind of familiar. Are you some kind of cop?"

"Have you seen him in the exhibit upstairs before?"

"Are you suggesting that I have nothing better to do than stand around in museums all day?" He tried on an indignant expression, then discarded it with a shrug. "You *do* work for MOMA, don't you? You saw me here before."

"You're making spontaneous confessions, Mr. DeBronk." She wanted to strangle him. "I don't care if you live in the museum. Can you help me by answering my question straight, or am I wasting my time?"

"Who is he? I *swear* I know his face."

"His name is Jonathan Hornebom. He's—"

"That's *Hornebom?* You mean Hornebom the crying-clown painter?"

"He's a painter, yes—"

DeBronk literally slapped his knee as he laughed. "I don't believe it."

"What's so funny?" She felt a protectiveness, of her case, of her client.

"You know those wide-eyed dogs and mimes and little ragamuffin kids, you *must* know them. He's just, like, the worst painter in the history of the twentieth century. I can't believe that's really him. I thought he was dead."

"Well, I guess not. Assuming we're talking about the same man."

"There couldn't be two. God." He shook his head.

"I guess I'm not too familiar with contemporary art," Harriet said.

"This would be more like familiar with contemporary dentist's offices," said DeBronk. "I can't believe a guy like that would show his face around here. Or want to. I mean, what do you think he was *seeing* up there?"

"I'd like very much to know."

"So what's the deal, why are you following him?"

"I'm not really at liberty to discuss it. And I should go. Here's my card. Please get in touch if you think of anything useful." She stood up.

"Is this your home phone? Can I see you again?"

"Leave a message."

"What are you doing tonight?"

4.

She saw him through his window, upstairs, from her place on the stoop across the street. The studio key was in her pocket now, but she didn't quite dare to investigate it with him upstairs and awake. Maybe after he was asleep.

She went to Seventh Avenue for cigarettes, then paced his block, smoking, for nearly an hour. Nothing. She spotted him behind the curtains a few times, passing between rooms, sitting reading in a chair. *You are boring, sir,* she reported to him in her head. *That'll be five thousand dollars. Or maybe you'd like to leave me your house in your will.*

On her fourth cigarette the sun finished setting. She was just about to head back to her apartment when Hornebom appeared at the top of his stoop, locking his door and tightening his scarf around his neck. She hurried around the corner, and watched as he headed for Seventh. In the dark she was more confident following close at his heels, and she tailed him to Waverly Place, where he went into the Coach House restaurant.

Here it was: her chance at his studio. She clutched the key in her pocket and half-ran back to Barrow.

She felt her excitement rise as she finally crossed the street and went through his gate. As a child her delight had been entering houses surreptitiously. Housesitting or babysitting, she'd always made copies of the neighbors' keys, and returned uninvited later to drink in the feel of their lives, the traces that lay everywhere.

She'd learned about adult life that way. Except the adult life she'd made for herself was nothing like that, contained none of those vulnerabilities. What she hadn't told the graduate student at the museum was that the office number *was* her home number; she skimped on bills by not keeping a phone upstairs. Her little apartment was nearly bare, would tell an intruder nothing.

She'd made her childhood spying her work, and she'd made her work her life.

She unlocked the basement door and slipped inside, into near-total darkness. Street light trickled in through the half-windows, and it occurred to Harriet suddenly that Hornebom had made an odd choice putting the studio in the basement: no natural light. If he owned the entire brownstone, why not the top floor? She remembered the graduate student laughing in the garden of the museum.

She groped along the wall for the light switch, and when she found it, flicked it on.

There stood Hornebom, wearing a madly smeared smock that reach the floor, and holding a dripping brush. He whipped around, exposed in the light, and she saw, in place of his head, the head of a monstrous bird, black eyes shining, beak narrowly open to reveal a pointed pink tongue nestled there, and curling at the sight of her. Then it was gone, her vision, and instead the human Hornebom bore down on her. He scumbled with his brush on the palette in his left hand, then raised it to her. "Do you need repainting, my dear?"

Her hand instinctively flicked the switch back down, as though the light had called him into being. He couldn't have been painting in the dark, went her wild thoughts, so he hadn't been there at all.

Her legs, finding this logic not quite satisfactory, carried her stumbling backwards, and out. She turned and ran through the gate, and across the street.

A woman was walking a small dog, and woman and dog looked up at Harriet as she fled the house. The street was quiet, and astonishingly normal. Harriet looked back; the basement was dark, of course, and there was no way of knowing if someone was inside.

Harriet stopped and looked back. The dogwalker passed; nobody came out of the basement studio.

Face burning with confusion and anger, Harriet half-walked, half-ran back to the Coach House. There was Hornebom at a table in the back, sipping fussily from a glass of wine, looking near the end of his meal. She turned away an urge to burst in and demand an explanation, instead ducked her head from the restaurant window and hurried home, suddenly terrified, and chilled to her heart by the night wind.

As she let herself into her building she heard the phone ringing behind her office door. She went into her office, and listened as her answering machine picked up the call.

"Hi, it's Richard DeBronk...we talked today, and I was just wondering, even though I don't really have any useful information for you, I mean about the crying-clown man, whether you might want to have a drink with me or something later tonight, or if tonight's not good—"

She grabbed the phone and switched off the machine. "Hi. Where do you want to meet?"

"Oh, hello. You're there. I, uh, I guess I didn't think of a place. I wasn't actually expecting—"

"White Horse Tavern. It's on Hudson and Eleventh."

"Wow, great, I guess you probably need some time—"

"I'll be there in ten minutes. Where are you coming from?"

"Chelsea, no problem, I'll be there soon. Uh, great."

Harriet was cold and afraid, the universe having opened up a gap she couldn't begin to account for. Her fear made her jump at an invitation she would otherwise ignore. Within half an hour she had herself shrouded in the almost medieval coziness and gloom of the White Horse, bolstered from within by Irish coffee, and enveloped in the loopy, discursive talk that was looking to be Richard DeBronk's trademark.

5.

"—original dissertation topic was the Freudian content of Max Ernst's work, the interrelations between some of his imagery and specific case studies in Freud, right? Good solid research topic, you know? I mean, the Surrealists all worked with dream imagery, automatic writing, they all loved pseudoscientific techniques—so it's not a revolutionary thesis, but I'm *explicating* the details, nailing it down, right? Art history departments are built on this kind of stuff, there's thesis work like this piled up to the ceiling; they give you your assistant professorship and then burn the dissertation to keep warm.

"So I was just digging around, verifying dates of paintings and collages so nobody could screw me up questioning the lines of influence and stuff—with historical assertions, it's like proving plagiarism in court, you have to demonstrate *access*. The connections can't just seem fertile from our vantagepoint, it has to have been at least *possible* that it would occur to the people involved. Okay, so I was working on sources for Ernst's collage novels—you've seen Max Ernst's collage novels, right?"

"Uh, no."

"Oh, God, you've got to, they're great. *The Hundred Headless Woman*, and *Une Semaine de Bonte*, which translates to something like 'One Week of Kindness.' They're these pictorial novels made up of collages—well, at least everybody *thinks* they're collages, but I'll get to that. Anyway, they're all these really striking images of people with rooster heads, lion heads, Easter Island-statue heads, and they're all in these domestic melodrama situations, performing these bizarre acts on each other. It's this vision of the world as a surreal nightmare, an endless series of revelations of the monstrous things just under the surface. So you can see why it relates so well to Freud—it's like Ernst is exposing the 'unconscious' reality."

"I follow."

"Well, okay, so it's widely asserted that Ernst's source material for these pictures, these *hundreds* of collages, was woodcut illustrations from Victorian pulp magazines and children's books, right? Because they *look* like those kinds of illustrations, everybody just made this assumption. Only a handful of the Ernst originals even exist—what everybody's working from are the published books. Well, I went back to the originals, I dug them out of some private collections, and I discovered something very weird: they're original engravings."

"Maybe you've lost me."

"They're not cut up and pasted together. You can't find any seams. What's passing for original collages are single, engraved images. If some kind of combining of elements ever occurred, it was at some earlier stage, and then Ernst, for no apparent reason, painstakingly reproduced his collages as original engravings. And nobody has any of the earlier versions, the actual collages. But anyway, that's not even the weirdest thing."

"Okay, I'm baited. What's the weirdest thing?"

"The presumed sources don't exist. The images originate with Ernst. No illustrations anywhere correspond to any part of any collage. I've wasted six months searching every possible archive, and I'm sure now. *The 'collages' have no sources.*"

DeBronk couldn't mask the triumph on his face, didn't even really try.

"This is a big deal," Harriet suggested tentatively.

"This is a *huge* deal. This is my career being made. Because discoveries like this aren't just lying around everywhere."

"So—the object in the case, at the museum—?"

"Well, now I'm trying to track down the real process, the methods Ernst used to create these images that he pretended were collages. He didn't own engraving tools of that type during the years the collage novels appeared. I've opened up huge mysteries about his process, his motives, and I want to try to solve some of that myself, present a finished package when I drop this bombshell, you know?

"Just before the collage novels appeared, Ernst created the object in the case, the 'Bird Camera.' There are numerous sketches for it in his notebooks—unlike a lot of the famous Surrealist objects, it wasn't just tossed off. It's a very complicated design. The plans for it have been generally regarded as a sort of elaborate hoax, a pretense that it had some function. That kind of coy crypto-science is very typical of the Surrealists. So everyone's just always assumed that it was a nonfunctional object, a pretend machine. But after Ernst created 'Bird Camera' he didn't sell it, wouldn't let it out of his studio. He even took it with him when he traveled, and it's a pretty bulky object."

"You think—"

"I'm sure of it. It's an image-fabrication machine, some weird unique design that Ernst came up with. The collages began appearing right after the 'Bird Camera' was finished."

"Can you prove it?"

"The museum won't let me near it. It's on loan from a museum in France—Ernst had to leave it behind when he fled the war. It'll be in New York for two more weeks, then back to Paris. You know, it's insured for millions of bucks, it's fragile as hell—all that stuff is, because the Surrealists weren't really sculptors, they just threw their things together. And I'm just a nobody graduate student. If I tell them why I want to see it I blow my scoop."

"Wow."

"Yeah, wow. You want another drink?"

He went to the bar and brought back two more Irish coffees. "Decaf, don't worry. So—now you."

"What?"

"Your turn. You have to tell me what you were doing there, at the museum. Your card says 'Investigator,' but I don't even know what that means."

Harriet was brought unexpectedly back to Hornebom. She wondered if Richard DeBronk could see her stiffen.

"I'm a researcher," she said. "Like you. Sometimes it involves...footwork, Hornebom led me to the museum. I still don't know what he was doing there, but I'll find out."

DeBronk made a face. "C'mon. Context, context. Why are you following the crying-clown man?"

Harriet sighed, and some of the tightness in her chest eased. "He hired me. It's an...unusual case. He's been suffering blackouts. And somebody's changing his paintings."

"That can only be a good thing," said DeBronk, grinning.

"Well, he doesn't think so. He hired me to investigate...."

"And?"

"I don't know. I went to his studio tonight, while he wasn't there. And...something was wrong."

"His studio? You have the key to his studio?"

She nodded.

He put his hand on her arm. "Take me there—"

"No!"

He put his hands together, pleadingly. "I promise not to tell anyone. But it's irresistible, it's too funny. I have to see it. Please."

"No. Stop. I don't want to talk about this anymore. I shouldn't—it's a breach that I told you anything."

"Sorry."

She shivered. Too much alcohol, too much caffeine. Too many questions. "Listen. Thanks for calling. It was interesting hearing your story. I've got to get to bed."

6.

Harriet switched on the television to drown out her thoughts as she fell asleep. She caught the end of the opening credits of the Midnight Movie—"Directed by Alfred Hitchcock"—as she climbed into bed. Perfect. She built a fort of pillows and blankets around her and settled in to watch.

It wasn't one she'd seen. A classic Hitchcock icy blonde and a hunkish hero were flirting in a pet shop.

An amiable enough opening, but Harriet knew Hitchcock. Sure enough, the situation quickly darkened—a possessive mother had her claws in the hero. A pair of lovebirds were purchased at the pet shop by the blonde, intended as a gift for the hunk, but undeliverable—a symbol of something, Harriet was sure.

Then real trouble began. The lovebirds began to swell and deform, bursting the bounds of the wire cage, until they were the shape and size of men cloaked in feathery three-piece suits. They shook themselves loose of the shards of cage like chicks freeing themselves of eggshells, cocked their heads briefly at one another and then climbed through the frame of Harriet's television set, and into her bedroom.

"Mademoiselle Welch," said the slimmer of the two birds. "We must speak with you."

"Interloper, meddler, hypocrite," said the stout one.

Harriet tried to rise from her bed, and found that somehow she couldn't. Tried to speak, and found herself voiceless.

"Breton is rather upset. He feels you are interfering with the development of a most promising pupil," said the slim one.

"Hornebom must be left alone," said the stout one. "You are not to investigate the case of Hornebom. To continue is punishable by excommunication from all you hold most dear."

"My name is Eluard," said the slimmer bird. "Don't let Breton upset you, he's merely saying how important it is—"

"We'll have you thrown to the sparrows!" Breton squawked.

It's the good bird/bad bird routine, Harriet thought.

"It is crucial, in selecting an investigation," said Eluard, "that you not inadvertently disrupt another, perhaps more crucial investigation already underway. We trust your error was in the nature of an oversight—"

"The sparrows that rend and devour!"

"To investigate birds you must become a bird," said Eluard.

"Creatures that live to shred hope!"

"Sleep now, Mademoiselle," said Eluard, nudging Breton back toward the television. "You've been warned."

7.

Harriet woke up angry. Hornebom was playing with her, and she resented it. Her idiotic dream was galling confirmation of her own susceptibility to his trick, his stunt, whatever it was he'd pulled off in the studio. In the bright light of morning it was clear to her that it had been nothing more than a clever special effect. The question was, What was the odd little man up to? What motive did he have for involving her in his games?

She'd find out, that was for sure.

She dressed and went out, grabbed coffee and a donut on Greenwich Avenue, and got to Barrow just in time to see Hornebom hurrying down the stoop, his collar up around his neck, his gaze darting nervously up and down the street yet seeming not to take her in.

She hesitated as he scurried up the street toward Seventh. Her urge to confront him vied with her curiosity, and lost; she trailed a safe distance behind.

Half an hour later she followed him into the "Anxious Furniture" exhibition and watched as he planted himself in front of "Bird Camera."

After fifteen or twenty minutes she approached him, partly just out of boredom with the alternative.

"Mr. Hornebom," she said, stepping up behind him, "we need to talk."

He turned and stared at her with a look of horror, and then darted away.

"Wait a minute—" she said, and took off after him, ignoring the stares she drew.

Hornebom made straight for the nearest guard, a stout black man stuffed like a sleeping bag into his gray polyester uniform. "Help me, please. This woman has been following me."

"Hmmm?" The guard roused slowly to Hornebom's frantic request. "She botherin' you?"

"I want you to arrest her," Hornebom said as Harriet arrived.

"Her? I ain't no cop," said the guard.

"What is this, Hornebom?" said Harriet. "Don't pretend—"

"Please, sir, help." Hornebom cowered from Harriet. "She won't leave me alone."

They were beginning to draw attention away from the nearest object, sugar cubes trapped in a wicker cage.

"This is ridiculous," said Harriet. "He *hired* me—"

"I've never seen her before," said Hornebom. "But, as you see, she's quite insistent. Please—"

Another guard, a middle-aged woman, stepped through the circle forming around them. "Let's get her out of here," she said. Harriet became suddenly conscious of the fact that Hornebom, in his suit and gloves and carefully combed white hair, looked every bit the helpless Uptown victim, while she, in her torn sweatshirt and gray Adidas, probably appeared thuggish.

The black guard put his hand on her arm.

"We can hold her for the police if you want," he said to Hornebom. "But you gonna have to stick around to make a statement. The museum don't have no charges to press, we'd just kick her out."

"I'll press charges myself," said Harriet. "I've got Hornebom's personal check in my desk. I'm *working* for him."

"Keep it down," said the first guard. "This a museum. You can argue it out when the cops get here."

"Okay, people," said the female guard. "Back to the show." The two of them steered Harriet back through the crowd, toward the lobby. Hornebom scurried after. They pushed through a door marked

"Personnel" to a tiny room where a third guard, an overweight man with a pink, bloated nose, sat at a desk with coffee and newspaper.

"We gotta sit on these two," said the first guard, jerking a thumb at Hornebom. "He wants to press charges." He pushed Harriet toward a chair against the wall.

"What a day," groaned the guard with the pink nose.

The female guard pushed the door closed, but just as quickly it pushed back open, and Richard DeBronk popped in. "Excuse me," he said.

"Personnel only," said the guard with the pink nose.

"Richard—" started Harriet.

"I think I can clear this up for you if you'll give me a minute," said Richard, grabbing the hand of the guard at the desk and shaking it vigorously. "Doctor DeBronk. I'm in charge of the outpatient clinic at St. Belfort's."

"Should I get a cop now?" said the female guard.

"There's no need for a cop," said DeBronk. "This is a misunderstanding between two patients, two very *unstable* patients. I assigned Harriet and Jonathan a museum trip today, and it's one hundred percent *my* fault if they created some kind of problem."

Harriet groaned. She could tolerate DeBronk rescuing her—barely—but this performance was getting a little campy.

Hornebom began to turn red. "I see no reason why—this preposterous—"

DeBronk put a warning finger in the air. "Now, Jonathan. Why don't you run along, and we'll see you

back at the residence. You shouldn't let Harriet pro-
voke you so easily. Here—this nice lady will help you
find your way downstairs." He stage-winked at the
female guard, and nodded broadly at Hornebom, who
could only bluster incoherently.

The pink-nosed guard opened the drawer of the
desk and took out a bottle of Pepto-Bismol and
poured from it into his coffee.

"There you go, that's good," said DeBronk, nudging
the female guard and Hornebom back through the door.

"What about her?" said the first guard, looking at
Harriet. Harriet stuck her tongue out at him.

"She can be a little tricky," said DeBronk. "I probably ought to re-hypnotize her—"

"Jesus Keeerist," said the guard with the pink nose.

"Okay, never mind. Here, do you need me to sign
something?"

"We gotta 'incident' form—"

"Let me save you the paperwork. Harriet, you sit
still. Let me fill that out for you, sir. My apologies for
all this trouble."

He went to the desk and took the form away from
the guard. "This pen doesn't work—" He dug in the
drawer, knocked the newspaper from the desktop,
and mixed a sequence of profuse apologies to the
guards with stern admonitions to Harriet not to move
a muscle—"remember what happened the day you got
loose at the zoo...." The guards rolled their eyes.
Finally he signed the bottom of the form with a flour-
ish—"R. DeBronk, Ph.D.—that's 'Piled Higher and

Deeper', hah hah"—came out from behind the desk, and took Harriet's arm.

And out they went. Harriet tugged free as they left the museum and rushed to the street corner, looking for Hornebom. The river of cabs attested to his likely easy escape. DeBronk caught up with her a minute later.

"I'm going to kill him," she said. "First I'm going to make him tell me what the hell he's up to, and then I'm going to kill him. Did you see—"

DeBronk nodded. "I'd just gotten there when you went up to him," he said. "I caught the whole thing."

They walked back to the portico of the museum.

"He's trying to make me a pawn in some game he's running," she said. "But he picked wrong. I'm going to nail him."

DeBronk nodded. "If there's anything to nail. He seems kind of out of it to me."

"An act. Trust me."

He smiled. "I do, actually."

"What's that supposed to mean—Hey, speaking of *acts*. What *was* all that crap?"

"Ulterior motives."

"You're quite the little bullshit artist, Doctor DeBronk."

"Thank you."

"Don't take it as a compliment until you stop bullshitting, please. What ulterior motives? Are you flirting with me?"

"Well," he said, grinning lasciviously, "there is a

palmed set of museum keys in my pocket." He jingled his loot. "But that doesn't mean I'm not glad to see you."

8.

"—you have to help me, Harriet, I can't do it alone—"

She and DeBronk were in her office talking, over sandwiches and coffee, when the door buzzer sounded.

"Yes?" she said into the intercom.

"Miss Welch? It's Jonathan Hornebom. May I speak with you?"

She looked at DeBronk, who shrugged. "Just a minute," she said, and clicked the intercom off.

"You can't be here," she said. "After what happened, it can't turn out that I know you. It guts my case against him if he recognizes you from the museum, and thinks we're collaborating."

"So hide me."

"Hide you. Is this what it's always like to hang out with you, DeBronk?"

"Hey, you're the one with the comic-book career."

"Shut up and get in the closet."

She buzzed Hornebom in and slid the sandwiches into her desk drawer. He opened the door to her office and she said, "Sit down."

He sat, meekly. "It's probably too soon, I realize. But I couldn't help wondering if you had—some sort of update. Any information at all, regarding the past two days."

"I might."

"Oh, good. I've been—there's been more changes. In the paintings."

"I'm sure."

"Well—oh, dear. Do I need to bring our account up to date?" He pulled out his checkbook and pen.

"That's not exactly the problem, Mr. Hornebom. Before you fill that out I need to ask you a couple of questions."

"Of course."

"I'm not necessarily in a position to protect you if what I uncover is evidence of criminal activity on your part, or even criminal *intent*. Do you understand that?"

"Oh, God, what have I done?"

"Just answer my question, please."

"I understand." He sank his head into his gloved hands.

"Okay. The second thing is that I'm no more interested in playing victim than I am accomplice or accessory. In the latter regard I *might* find a way to turn a blind eye to things—but if you fuck with *me* I'll take you down, and fast. Got that?"

The sudden rough language was a calculated effect, and Harriet saw it work. Hornebom gaped at her, slack-jawed.

"Please tell me what I've done," he finally managed.

"Please finish answering my questions. What were you doing at the museum today?"

"The museum? I've no idea—I've no memory of today. That's the problem, you must believe me. Please!"

Harriet made a face, stalling. Finally she said, "Go ahead and write me a check—make it for two more days."

"Yes, of course." He scribbled it out, staining his glove with ink, and tore it from the book. As he handed it to her he spoke in a near-whisper. "Will you tell me, please, what you know of my activities—"

"You've been visiting the museum. And something's definitely wrong with your studio. That's my report for today. Go home, Mr. Hornebom. I'll call you when my work is complete."

"Please—"

"I don't want to interfere until the pattern has become clear," she said, and as she said it Eluard's warning from her dream echoed in her head: *important not to disrupt another, more important investigation—*

Hornebom nodded in a deflated way, and went to the door. When he was gone, DeBronk came out of the closet and sat in the seat across the desk from Harriet.

"He doesn't remember," he said.

"Or it's a superb act."

"Maybe you'd better fill me in on this now."

She did, from the beginning, without skipping anything but the idiotic dream. "Well," he said when she'd finished. "It's obvious what you need."

"What?"

"Same thing I need—a partner. If he's playing some game, he's counting on your being alone. If there's two of us, one following him, the other staking out the studio—"

"Whoa. Slow down."

9.

Harriet didn't finish losing the argument until they were outside the darkened rear entrance to the museum. She gave up when he began fumbling at the door with the stolen keys. She pushed his hand away and whispered: "Wait!"

"I told you, I'm going in with or without you."

"Whatever. But you can't just break in like that. Jeez. Here, you need this."

He stared at the device she pulled out of her bag. "What's that?"

"Well, the main security system's probably motion detectors. On all the floors and maybe in the displays, too. This thing averages out the kind of motion disturbances that trigger alarms. Like a steadicam. So it'll cloak us from that kind of system."

"Wow."

"Of course, if they've got something else we're dead meat."

"Oh."

They crept inside. No alarms sounded.

The halls were half-lit, eerily so. Empty, the lobby

was oppressively huge, and crossing it Harriet felt exposed, like a cat in a cathedral. They stopped at the frozen escalator and listened; surely there were overnight guards. Just as surely, in Harriet's experience, those guards were sequestered in some room like the one she'd been taken to earlier that day, and surrounded with some combination of booze, cigarettes, radio, cards, or pornographic magazines, if not all of the above.

Hearing nothing, they tiptoed up the inert steps, two floors, to "Anxious Furniture." In the gloom of the emptied museum, Harriet was suddenly aware of the strange, vibratory power of the pieces in the exhibition. Ogled by throngs, the objects had been reduced to monkeys in cages. Now they were somehow predatory, feeding on the darkness and silence and leaking it back out in purified form.

DeBronk unlocked the case containing his and Hornebom's mysterious favorite. He plucked "Bird Camera" off its perch and eased it through the narrow opening in the back of the case, then wrapped it up in his coat making a bulky, obvious bundle.

Richard looked at the empty spot in the case, between the metronome and the teacup, guiltily. Then, suddenly inspired, he handed "Bird Camera" to Harriet. He snuck out into the hall, and came back with a small red fire extinguisher.

"Cigarette," he whispered. She gave him one. He stuck it into the nozzle at the top of the fire extinguisher, to which it imparted a jaunty continental air, and put the new object in the case in place of the missing Ernst.

On the second floor they froze, hearing noises from the lobby. Someone on patrol. They waited until the sounds trickled away, then slipped back through the lobby and out, unharassed, booty intact.

They ferried it in a cab back to her office. DeBronk unwrapped it on her desk and then sank into her chair, hollow-eyed.

"What?" said Harriet.

"We stole it. I can't believe it."

"Yeah, we stole it."

"One of the major pieces in Ernst's career. This is like the most fatal thing I could possibly do in my profession. I can't believe it's sitting here. We took it out of the museum."

"What, are you going to fall apart on me now? You had to, you *said* you had to. Christ."

"It's just—"

"Here." She opened her bottom drawer and handed him a bottle of whiskey.

"Wow," he said dreamily.

"What now?"

"You really keep whiskey in your desk. Like a private eye."

She rolled her eyes.

He shook his head. "You're just so cool." He took a slug from the bottle. "Okay. Paper, paper, I need paper." She opened the upper drawer and pulled out a few sheets of her stationery. "Scissors. Need to cut it down a little—" She supplied scissors. He took another bolt from the whiskey bottle, and set to slimming the paper. He checked it against the width of "Bird Camera," then cut off another sliver.

"Okay, here goes," he said, manipulating the knobs tucked under the cannon end of the sculpture.

"You know how it works?" Harriet was the nervous one now. What if they destroyed it?

"I memorized the notebook pages where he designed this thing," said DeBronk. "They were all I had—until now." His tongue stuck out of one side of his mouth as he eased the fitted paper into the maw of the press, then flicked the knob underneath the right-hand wheel.

There was a flash at the mouth of the cannon, as though it had fired. A lick, a grinding of gears, and the paper was drawn into the heart of the machine.

A pause, then the paper rolled smoothly out the other end, like Polaroid film. DeBronk hurried around the desk and caught it as it fell loose.

The engraving was in the style of a nineteenth-century woodcut illustration, but it showed the corner of Harriet's office. Harriet was just at the edge of the frame, her shoulder at the bottom of the left corner, the side of her head and ear visible along the left edge.

Hovering in the space of the room, and filling the center of the engraving, were the two birds from Harriet's dream, Breton and Eluard. Eluard was smoking a pipe, and Breton was holding a bright, metallic-looking sphere which intersected the lobe of Harriet's ear like a hoop earring.

"It's incredible!" said DeBronk. "It's an original Ernst! An original *posthumous* Ernst!"

Harriet stared. "It's a photograph," she said. "That's me."

"Not a photograph, exactly. A Max-o-graph, for Max Ernst. He's like another Leonardo. God, this is so great."

Harriet couldn't find voice to express her apprehension about what the "Maxograph" revealed.

DeBronk began excitedly cutting more paper to size and loading it into the tray at the back of the device. "Do one of me." He aimed the cannon at himself. "Push the button."

She turned the knob, and "Bird Camera" snapped another shot. DeBronk with the head of a crocodile, wearing a top hat, and holding a figurine of a naked Aphrodite.

In the air over his head flew a small black sparrow.

"It's like a Surrealist party toy," said DeBronk. "The conceit is that it uncovers psychical reality, takes a picture of the subconscious world. He must have programmed the etching blades with thousands of images. And it combines them to match what the cannon lens is aimed at. It's brilliant."

"Let's—let's take a Maxograph of someone else."

"Okay. Outside." He scooped up "Bird Camera" and they went out onto the street. Holding it at chest level, he aimed it at a young couple walking on the other side of the street.

A giant rooster walking an ape on a leash, in a hail of disembodied breasts. The buildings behind showed a variety of nightmarish dramas half-hidden behind the window curtains.

"Wow, he's even got it programmed so Loplop is in each picture," said DeBronk.

"What's Loplop?"

"Not what, who. Loplop was a bird character, sort of Ernst's imaginary alter ego. He put Loplop in a lot of the collages."

Not all of those birds are named Loplop, Harriet wanted to say, but the words didn't come out.

"Harriet, I'm going to be famous. It's okay that we broke in, nobody will care."

"I'm happy for you."

"What—what's the matter?"

"Nothing. Nothing, just I need a favor, okay? No questions."

"Sure."

"We have to take a picture, a Maxograph, of Hornebom. Right away."

He smiled and shrugged. "Sure, sounds hilarious. Let's go."

She bit her lip. They walked to Barrow Street. Hornebom's studio lights were on. Harriet stopped DeBronk at the stoop across the street. "His house first."

"The famous Hornebom residence, exposed by the all-seeing 'Bird Camera,' " he announced, and turned the knob. Flash.

Water poured out of the windows of the upper floors, to meet the flames licking out of the windows of the basement studio, producing clouds of steam that drifted off and mingled with the clouds of the night sky. The moon, above, was being mothered like an egg by an enormous vulture.

Harriet shuddered, then caught herself. She had to know. "I want—I want to catch him painting," she said. "With that thing."

"You can include the Maxograph with your report, as evidence," DeBronk suggested merrily. They slipped across the street and through his gate, and went to the ground-level window of the basement studio. Harriet peered over the top. There he was, back turned, shoulders draped in the spattered smock. She pointed. DeBronk aimed "Bird Camera."

Something, some noise or disturbance in the air, alerted him. As the cannon flashed, he turned and saw them. "Run!" Harriet whispered, and, in the grip of some unnatural fear, turned and fled herself.

DeBronk caught up with her as she unlocked the door to her office. "Look," he said, holding out the Maxograph.

It was Hornebom with the maniacal bird's head she'd hallucinated the night before.

The painting he was working on was of Harriet herself, her huge eyes flooding with tears.

Before she could utter a word, the phone in her office rang. Suddenly sure it was Hornebom, she pulled the door shut again, not even wanting to hear him record a message, not even wanting to enter a room he'd so recently inhabited.

"Upstairs," she said, half gasping.

DeBronk followed her into her apartment, and while she was carefully locking the door he put "Bird Camera" on her counter and spread the nightmarish Maxographs out on her kitchen table.

"No," she said when she turned and saw them. She scooped them up and put them in a drawer with a pile of folded tablecloths.

"What's the matter?"

"Nothing. I just don't want to look at them—at night."

"You're acting strange."

"Yes, I know." She launched herself toward him, to shut him up, and for other reasons. Kill two birds, she caught herself thinking.

The kiss started badly, their teeth clacking together, but lasted long enough that they put the mistakes behind them.

"Wow," he said.

"You should get rid of that stupid little beard," she said. "It makes you look like a boy with a beard."

"But if I shave it off, then I'll just look like a boy."

"No, if you shave it off you'll look like a young, um, guy."

"Fellow, you mean."

"Young man. Young guy, dude, something. Not a boy with a beard."

They kissed some more.

"I thought you were going to complain about the scratchiness," he said.

"No, I like that. But it looks stupid."

They went into her room and lay on the bed together. Suddenly he sat up. "Just one more Maxograph," he said. "I have to do the television—"

Harriet sighed.

"Please." He kissed her, then pulled away and got "Bird Camera" out of the kitchen. "Something Ernst couldn't have imagined, something that didn't exist—" He switched her television on. *Star Trek.*

"That should do it," she said.

He got back on the bed beside her and aimed the cannon eye. Flash.

Kirk and Spock in each other's arms, Bones glowering in the background. The tricorder in Spock's hand had been changed into a small gray dove, which he held to the captain's breast.

"Spock, Kirk, I never knew," said DeBronk.

"Seems like a hint," said Harriet. "You know, 'Birds do it, bees do it, even Kirk and Spock do it'—mmphh."

He kissed her, putting "Bird Camera" and the new Maxograph on her bedside table.

Then, for a long while, only the sound of their breathing and the babble of the television.

"I wonder," he whispered. "If someone took a Maxograph of us now...." Their clothes were all on the floor.

"Probably you'd turn out to be Hornebom," she said. "So let's skip it—ooh...."

Finally they were still as well as quiet. They lay together on the pillows as the television blared: "Now, for the first time offered to the general public, never before available, a unique six-CD package: Goof Hits of the Fifties, Sixties, Seventies, Eighties, and Nineties! That's right, all these hits—" As the voice listed songs, a snippet of each played underneath. "— 'Flying Purple Eater,' 'The Streak,' 'Convoy,' 'Rainy Day Women #12 and 35,' 'Surfin' Bird'—"

At that moment a flock of birds rushed through the television screen into the room. They landed on the floor and grew into a scowling, feather-suited jury, Eluard and Breton at the fore.

"Doesn't she know about the Bird?" said one. "I thought by now everyone had been informed regarding the Bird."

"She should know about the Bird," said Eluard. "We told her that Bird was the Word."

"Yes, in the Beginning was the Bird," said another.

"We must exact our punishment," said Breton.

"Dada ooh mow mow," said a bird in the rear.

Harriet found again that she couldn't move or speak. She and DeBronk were trapped, naked and immobile in the bed.

"Perhaps we should make our objections more clear," said Eluard.

"Perhaps we should rend flesh from bone," said Breton.

"Please, Aragon, will you silence Breton. Tzara, where is Tzara? Ah, Tristan, please, if you will, elucidate for this Adam and Eve the gravity and direness of the situation."

A bird with spectacles stepped up to the bed. "You must understand that we are only the Sons of the Bird. The True Bird is everywhere, and he is far more powerful, more dangerous than we handful of Sons. For so many years the Bird Who Is Everywhere ruled unopposed, and his was a cruel reign, spasmodic in its violence, brutal in its indifference.

"Then we Sons were born, out of the ashes of the crudest, bloodiest birth spasms the Bird had ever known. There had been Sons before, but scattered, isolated, helpless to sound the alarm. We were the first Sons to band as we did, though indeed we too were helpless in the face of the Ravages of the Bird, the Ravages that were to come.

"Among us Sons was one known as Loplop, Bird Superior. He, more than any other, could glimpse the Bird Who Is Everywhere. His unerring finger found the Bird out, warned of its claws."

"Loplop must live again!" said Breton.

"You must resist interfering any further," concluded Tzara somberly.

"How can they be trusted? You see they have His camera. How will Hornebom find it here?"

"It is true," said the one called Aragon. "It is not enough now that they desist. Damage is done."

"Take her hostage!"

"But this could be called advantageous," said Eluard. "Bunglers they may be, but they freed His instrument from its tomb, they returned it to use—which Hornebom himself could not do."

"It must be delivered," said Aragon. "Take the man, leave her with the camera. When it is delivered, she shall have him back. When we have our Loplop, Eve shall have her Adam."

"Revenge, excommunication!" shrieked Breton.

"No," said Tzara. "It is enough that we take him. Away, now."

The birds rose, flapping, into the air of Harriet's bedroom, and as they swirled through the air in a vortex toward the television, DeBronk rose up from the bed and shrank, until he circled away with them into the drain of the screen.

The cyclone of birds left not a single feather. Harriet fell asleep.

10.

Harriet didn't want to think about what had gone so wrong that DeBronk left without "Bird Camera" or, from the look of things, most of his clothes. The utter jerk. She stumbled out of her bedroom and into the kitchen.

She opened the tablecloth drawer and stared at the stack of Maxographs. In the light of day the images were unconvincing, and she couldn't imagine what had scared her so much the night before. They were clever, the device that had produced them was clever, certainly, but it was clever nonsense, and she was tired of it. Art. She was swearing off art now, generally. And swearing off clever, nonsensical art historians in particular.

She made coffee and considered her situation. The sculpture in her bedroom was stolen property, important stolen property. She would have to get it back. And her client was bullshit. She needed to drop him. She suddenly wondered if Richard DeBronk was Hornebom's colleague. It would explain a lot. DeBronk had suggested that it would take two to *uncover* Hornebom's hijinks, but wasn't it equally true that it would take two to *produce* them?

The only thing that kept her from returning the uncashed check in her wallet was…well, the uncashed check in her wallet. Her account cried for it. She'd contracted to trail him for a third day and deliver a report, and if she did so she could rightfully keep the money.

One more day of surveillance wouldn't hurt. It might even clear up a few things.

For Harriet, shadowing was therapeutic. It placed her in her deepest, truest self, her pleasure in stealth, her core of ancient curiosities.

She picked up Hornebom at his door and followed him to a café for coffee and newspaper. She found her own copy of the paper while he was engrossed in his; no mention of the missing "Bird Camera."

He caught a cab, heading uptown, and she did the same, thinking: *Rerun.* Sure enough, Hornebom's cab pulled up at the museum. Harriet told her cabbie to stop.

Suddenly it hit her: *If they were working together, Hornebom wouldn't bother to come back up here. "Bird Camera" isn't here.*

A chink opened in her skepticism, and through it she glimpsed a horror-film sequence of images from the night before.

"Uh, Sixty-eighth Street and Lexington," she told the cabbie.

"What?"

"I changed my mind."

The cabbie shrugged, turned the wheel, and honked his way back into the flow of traffic.

She paid her fare and ran into the bustling lobby of the main building at Hunter College, working her way through mobs of students to the information desk.

"Graduate offices for the art history department," she said.

"409."

She went upstairs in the elevator, and in room 409 found the secretary for the department.

"I'm looking for a Richard DeBronk," she said.

"You'll have to wait in line."

"What do you mean?"

"Well, dear, he wouldn't ordinarily be around *here*. He's writing his dissertation—doesn't require that he appear at the department much. But he *is* teaching an undergraduate class across the street, and they've called twice this morning looking for him."

"He didn't show up?"

"If he did, they didn't let me know about it. Last I knew, the class was waiting for him."

"What's the room number?"

Harriet went downstairs and out, and into the annex across the street. She found his classroom just as the last of the students were giving up waiting.

"DeBronk didn't show up?" she asked.

"Nope."

"He's a flaky type, right? Does this often?"

"What are you, from the administration? He's never missed a class before."

Harriet's heart sank. DeBronk was a real person, with real responsibilities and connections in the world. Not just some capricious con man.

Where was he?

She went outside and caught a cab home. At her office door she paused, looked inside quickly to see if there were any phone messages. No. She rushed up to her bedroom, switched on the television, and began flipping channels. On channel nine a *Partridge Family* rerun was just starting. The opening sequence, a series of animated partridges hatching from eggs. But instead of the Partridge Family, the newborn birds turned into the cabal from Harriet's dream: Eluard, Breton, Tzara, Aragon, and several others. They smiled and waved as one by one they were introduced.

At the end of the sequence came the one continuing character who wasn't a Partridge, who wasn't hatched: the talented family's beleaguered, whining manager, played in today's episode by Richard DeBronk.

To add to the manager's usual humiliations at the hands of the Partridge children, DeBronk was naked. As the show opened, the monstrous birdmen were at their instruments, bobbing together as they played, Breton singing lead, a scabrous "Surfin' Bird" in a thick French accent.

DeBronk scurried around the perimeter, wringing his hands, his penis flapping, insisting hopelessly that they practice some other song.

Horrified, Harriet snapped the television off. She sat stunned for a minute, as the impossible truth sank in. Then she grabbed "Bird Camera," stuffed it into a shopping bag in the kitchen, and ran downstairs, and out.

At Barrow Street Hornebom was already back in his studio, wearing his spattered smock. She crossed the street and knocked on the window. He went on painting, his back to her. She let herself in with the key.

As she stepped into the studio there was a rush from the canvases lining the walls, and she was surrounded by a posse of sad-eyed children; looming, top-heavy homeless-person clowns; and puppy watchdogs with enormous, weepy eyes. They massed all around her, hemming her in, backing her toward the door. The puppies growled gently, the children murmured to themselves—"Is the nice lady a bird too?" "Where's my daddy?" "I just want to play house, but there's nothing but bullies on my block"—and the clowns chanted in singsong voices—"Gotta cheer *up* the birds, *they're* not nasty birds they're just *grumpy*, can't let 'em getcha down, uh, yeah, but who's the *lady* with the package? Don't want no birds in *here*, gotta make Mr. Hornebom happy, he's the *boss*, oh ho—"

Their gabbling rising to a roar, the clowns and puppies and children floated up to loom over Harriet, threatening to smother her with their marsh-mallow-soft bodies. She struck out at one and it burst like a balloon, spattering gobs of oil paint all over her arm.

"Hornebom!" Harriet shouted over the din. He went on frantically painting, tossing off new children and puppies and clowns who instantly rose from the canvas to join the barrage. "Hornebom! I have your report!"

"I don't need a report," he said without turning. "My situation is all too clear."

"What situation?" She swatted the forms away from her mouth and eyes.

"I went to the museum." He turned and looked at her accusingly. "Someone had stolen the bird detector I'd been coveting. The shock of it opened my eyes."

"I've got it for you, right here—"

"No, no my dear, I can see the birds all by myself now, I don't need it. I've been thrown back on my own resources, I understand now. The birds are everywhere. It's just me and my children, that's all I can count on." He smiled maliciously. "For instance, you my dear, I see that you are a bird, like all the others. How frightening that a few short days ago I was so blind as to walk into your nest and ask you for help. As though you could help me!"

He dashed off a pair of enormous, weepy disembodied eyes, which were so impatient to join the throng that they floated off the canvas by themselves before their maker could surround them with a clown.

Harriet pushed the forms away from her, but as they met the resistance of others pressing behind them they began to melt together, like soap bubbles, and form the beginnings of one huge clown, whose oil-paint hide was much thicker than that of his miniature brethren. "You're as much a bird as me," said Harriet. She began backing toward the door, overwhelmed, and wary of the gigantic clown in the making.

"It's no good trying to fool me now!" screamed Hornebom. The children and puppies and clowns began flowing directly off his brush and pouring toward her. "I see the birds, I see you! They're everywhere! It's only me, I'm all alone, only me and my children to save me! I see the birds!"

"There's one bird you haven't spotted," said Harriet. She elbowed the puppies away from the shopping bag and drew out "Bird Camera." One sheet of her stationery, cut to size by DeBronk, was left in the tray. She jostled the clowns between her and Hornebom, trying to clear an unobstructed view. The giant clown lay sprawled at her feet, embryonic, yet already struggling to its feet.

Flash!

The collage that emerged showed Hornebom with a beak. Good enough. Harriet charged into the mass of clowns and children and puppies and held the paper out to Hornebom. "Take it! Look!" Her body dripped with oil paint. The giant clown seized her legs.

Hornebom snatched the paper away from her.

He dropped his brush. The clowns and puppies and children all held where they stood, yipping and sniffling and chortling in melancholy voices.

Hornebom seemed to fade, his certainty gone. The paper he held grew larger, extended easel-legs to the floor, wooden ruler-arms outward, and a long easel-neck upward. The neck was topped with a small, round bird's head, with a comb like a rooster's.

"Finally," said the easel-bird. It shook itself with a clatter, then stepped over and kicked the giant clown away from Harriet's legs. "How do you do. My name is Loplop."

"Harriet Welch," said Harriet.

"Very good choice, mademoiselle, to turn the camera on my poor son. Thank you." The voice that issued from the little red bird's head atop the easel-body was soft and mannered, with a slight German accent.

Hornebom stood looking dumbfounded.

"Yes, Jonathan, you are my son. I am your father, though you never knew me. This is a wrong that must be righted. A bird that must be captured on canvas, so to speak."

"My father died in Germany," said Hornebom softly.

"No, your adoptive father died there. Your true father, Max Ernst, left your mother never knowing she was pregnant with you. He—I—moved often and quickly in that regard. Regrettable, perhaps. Max lived many years in France and America never knowing he had this son. But I, Loplop, came to know of your existence, your emigration to America, your...ah, career."

"Ernst or Loplop—which are you?" asked Harriet.

"Ah. Ernst was Loplop. His secret identity, his bird self, both horrible and wise. But when Ernst died I, Loplop, lived on."

"Why didn't you come forward sooner?"

"This is a rare freedom I enjoy now. When it is over I shall go back to the margins, trapped in museum depictions, flourishing occasionally in the seams between things, like the other Sons, but unable to speak aloud. I did what I could, I tried to direct his hand—"

"The altered paintings," said Harriet.

"Yes. I added a glimpse of the Bird to his soporific canvases."

"But the Birds," whispered Hornebom. "The terrible Birds."

"Yes, we are all terrible Birds," said Loplop. "I was the Bird when I treated your mother so badly, during that terrible time when all of Germany seemed endlessly Birds. But I painted what I saw. You have spent your life running from the Bird, and so the Bird is never named, never mastered."

Loplop turned to Harriet. "My son had a powerful Surrealist magic in him. Despite his never knowing his heritage, it knew itself in him. But he put it to very poor use. Jonathan is a reverse Icarus. His father equipped him with wings, but rather than fly too near the sun, he never left the ground." He scowled at the puppies and clowns and children, who were now beginning to scurry and melt back into the canvases that lined the walls of the studio.

Loplop took "Bird Camera" out of Harriet's hands. "My little toy. Jonathan won't need it now—you must return it to its place in the museum." He stilted over and put it into the shopping bag, then looked at a watch on his wooden wrist. "Hurry home now, you have to free your friend from the television. *Sesame Street* will be over in a few minutes."

"What about The Sons of the Bird?" asked Harriet.

"I'll see to that. Breton is a scoutmaster at heart, always checking and revoking memberships, slapping wrists and handing out medals. You mustn't take it too seriously."

He looked back at Hornebom, who stood hapless in the midst of his canvases, his eyes nearly as large as those he ceaselessly depicted.

"Please leave us," said Loplop. "I have many apologies to make, as a father." He paused, scowling. "And my son has equally many to make, as a painter."

11.

Their house is not exactly in the city, but the city can be seen from the nearby promenade. It's a part of Brooklyn Heights where it is possible to live in brownstones very much as lovely as Hornebom's, without living anywhere near Hornebom himself. Her success as an expert in museum and auction security, due in large part to her celebrated rescue of Max Ernst's "Bird Camera," permits her to run the agency at a remove. He still teaches, but not because he has to. There is not a single television in the entire house.

HOW I GOT
INSIPID:
AN AFTERWORD

These two stories share a few distinctions, and in some way can be seen as final evidence of a certain mode in my work—one otherwise entirely collected in my two short story collections, *The Wall of the Sky, The Wall of the Eye* (Harcourt Brace, 1997) and *Men and Cartoons* (Doubleday, 2004), and in the so-called novella (actually only 50 pages long), *This Shape We're In* (McSweeney's, 2000). The fact is, I'm an instinctive novelist. It's easy for me to digress and expand. Rigorously organized short stories are less native to me, more a learned discipline. When I first began writing stories I tended to produce what I'd call 'short novellas', like these two. Another way to describe this form, which usually involved a greater number of situations, characters, and motifs than the short story is usually thought capable of containing, is as a 'compacted novel.' Or, less generously, as a 'first chapter to an unwritten novel,' which is how many of them strike me, nowadays. They introduce dangerously much material in dangerously compacted form, then hurry to a frenzied conclusion.

All of the stories in *The Wall of the Sky, The Wall of the Eye* fit this description, with the exception of "Forever, Said the Duck." By the time of my second collection I'd learned to write a proper short story, with a reduced number of elements, handled in a manner proportionate to the form as it is traditionally practiced. In *Men and Cartoons* only "Access Fantasy" would qualify under this description; the remainder are "natural." I don't make the claim that these natural short stories are better, or even good, only that they're true to the tradition, whereas these compacted novels of mine remain (no matter how well they may sometimes work on their own terms) mock turtles, like the one with hooves and a calf's head in Lewis Carroll's *Alice*.

"The Insipid Profession of Jonathan Hornebom" was written in time to be included in my first collection. In fact, it was part of the original manuscript, until my editor at Harcourt, Michael Kandel, talked me out of it. I think he thought it was too cute. He also mentioned something about it being "tendentious about visual art," a remark that stung at the time, but which I'll admit was keen in naming that persistent tendency in my work (see: "Ad Man," "Mood Bender," "The Happy Prince," "Hugh Merrow," "K For Fake," *The*

Fortress of Solitude). While the book, sans "Insipid Profession," was in galleys, the story was nominated for a World Fantasy Award, a fact about which I teased Michael. It lost. The following year the whole collection, sans "Insipid Profession," was nominated for a World Fantasy Award. It won. Whether you'll conclude from this parable that I was wrong, or Michael Kandel was wrong, or the World Fantasy Award judging panel was (once? twice?) wrong, I can only guess.

"How We Got Into Town and Out Again" was, similarly, on the short list for inclusion in my second collection, *Men and Cartoons.* It was excluded by my own editorial eye, as schooled by Kandel and other editors I'd worked with. I liked the story in many respects, but it seemed a little too dependent on the research I'd done into 1930s dance marathons, and also a little tendentious on the subject of virtual reality, a bugaboo of mine after I'd lived through The Great Bay Area Virtual Reality Hype Of 1985-92 (the dates are approximate, and my own). You can see me arguing with *Wired Magazine* and Jaron Lanier and a lot of other jubilant proponents of a happy-future-without-bodies in stories like "Walking the Moons" and "Forever, Said the Duck" as well as in the novel *Amnesia Moon;* "How We Got in Town" was, I think, a culmination and end to that sequence.

So another, simpler way to look at this pair of stories is as the most ambitious of my shorter fictions *not* included in my first and second collections, in turn. For a long time there were no more stories like this, and then I wrote "This Shape We're In," in many ways the most compacted and impossible of them all. That will be the last, I suspect.

"Insipid Profession" was written as an elaborate parody of a Robert Heinlein novella, "The Impossible Profession of Jonathan Hoag." Heinlein's was a paranoid, solipsistic jape in the *Weird Tales* vein, nothing at all to do with extrapolation. I decided to smash it together with Max Ernst, Alfred Hitchcock, and the Trashmen's "Surfin' Bird," along with several other references I've now forgotten. And the lead character is, of course, Harriet the Spy, grown up. The story had some other title, also forgotten, until an editor, in the process of rejecting the piece, wrote me a worried letter to say I'd either consciously or unconsciously plagiarized the Heinlein. I retitled it to make the homage self-evident, but the incident was jangling, one of my earliest brushes with a confusion over the shades between "parody," "appropriation," "influence," "quotation" and "theft" that, in a world which makes room for Andy Warhol, Walt Disney, and Borges' "Don Quixote by Pierre Menard," still bedevils me. In preparing to write the story I read memoirs by Dorothea Tanning and Jimmy Ernst (what an industrious boy I was), and Michael Kandel may be right; likely too much of my research got onto the page. I like the museum at night, though.

"How We Got In Town and Out Again" appropriates Horace McCoy's (and Sydney Pollack's) *They Shoot Horses, Don't They?* in the cause, as I've said, of a slashing attack on the utopian assumptions surrounding the promotion of what was then called virtual reality. Of course, these days I live on the web as much as I do in my house, while back then I had not the faintest notion of what it was I was deriding so forcefully. Still, our pulsing, horny, rotting bodies eventually win all arguments—I'm hungry as I write this, and I need another cup of coffee, too—so I think I had enough ground to stand on. The story was my last appearance in both "Isaac Asimov's Science Fiction Magazine" and in *The Year's Best Science Fiction* series, and I think it's fair to say it was my last attempt to paint within those particular lines. It was a farewell not to the literature of the fantastic, but to the contemporary SF marketplace. It was written for the Sycamore Hill Writer's Conference, and those wonderful people deserve credit for keeping me honest, here and elsewhere.

Lastly, these two stories are also linked by my readiness to anchor the material of crime or mystery writing to my weird or futuristic premises, a combination which sustains my first novel, *Gun, With Occasional Music.* I don't think I ever noticed how often I was making this choice, which could also describe stories like "Hardened Criminals" and "The Happy Man" and "Access Fantasy." The further away you get from the stuff you leave behind, the more it all looks the same. Do I repeat myself? Let me stop here, then, before I do it again.

September, 2005